H(

A Finn Mc(

By Scott Langrel

Copyright©2012 by Scott Langrel

All Rights Reserved

This is a work of fiction. Any resemblance of characters to actual persons, living or dead, is purely coincidental.

Other books by Scott Langrel:

The Grass Monkey and Other Dark Tales

Skewed: A Collection of Uneasy Tales

To Mom and Dad, who did a really good job of raising me, considering what they had to work with.

Table of Contents

Prologue 4
Chapter One 11
Chapter Two 19
Chapter Three..26
Chapter Four..33
Chapter Five...40
Chapter Six...47
Chapter Seven 54
Chapter Eight 60
Chapter Nine..68
Chapter Ten 75
Chapter Eleven 84
Chapter Twelve..90
Chapter Thirteen..96
Chapter Fourteen...104
Chapter Fifteen...112
Epilogue..116
Preview of Shadows in the Sand: A Finn McCoy Paranormal Thriller 119

Prologue

If Alvin ever found the damn dog, he was going to kill it.

Well, probably not, since the sorry excuse for a canine had set him back three-hundred dollars, but the thought was appealing, nonetheless. It was well past lunch time, and Alvin was not a man known for missing meals. He had never been able to understand how some people could become so involved in an activity that they would skip a feeding. He'd worked with guys like that, back before he'd gotten his disability, and he had never trusted them. When the clock struck twelve, you dropped whatever you were doing and you went and ate your lunch. You had to have your priorities straight, and Alvin Hobbs figured his priorities were as straight as an arrow.

Hunting came in right below eating on Alvin's list, particularly coon hunting. There was nothing finer than the sound of a hound braying as it treed its quarry. On the flip side, there was nothing more frustrating than losing a dog, which was the reason Alvin was trampling around on Drover Mountain instead of sitting down to a bowl of beans or a corned beef sandwich. Blue, his newest acquisition, had failed to return with the others when he'd called them in this morning, and so far he'd been unable to find the stupid mutt. But three-hundred dollars was a lot of money, and Alvin would be damned if he was going to lose the dog, especially after the grief Wanda had given him about spending that much money in the first place.

Alvin stopped and called for the dog. Silence answered him. He was dead tired; he'd been up most of the night hunting, and he had hoped to be home in bed by now. He had another hunt planned for tonight, but if he didn't get any sleep, that would go out the window. Damn dog. Pete Fergouson had warned Alvin about buying dogs from Ol' Walt, but he had gone and done it anyway. Now he was paying for it.

The noon sun was bright and warm, causing Alvin to consider shedding some of his clothing. He was dressed for a nighttime hunt, not for traipsing about in the middle of the day. But he didn't want to be lugging stuff around with him; the terrain was steep and rocky here, and he was constantly slipping on the freshly-fallen leaves as he went. He'd left his gun locked in the truck for that very reason. He'd seen more than a few hunting accidents caused by people slipping and falling while holding a loaded gun. He had his .22 revolver on him, just in case he ran into a snake, but they generally weren't much of a problem this time of year.

He began to walk again, wondering how far he should go before giving up. Further up the slope, a rabbit broke cover and made a mad, zigzagging dash across the next rise. Alvin watched it go, his hopes of finding Blue starting to diminish. Maybe it would be better to just turn back. There was a good chance that someone would find the dog and return him to Alvin. He knew most of the other hunters in the area, and they would all know whose dog Blue was if they happened upon him. Besides, it wouldn't be the first dog he'd ever lost—though arguably the most expensive—and he was awfully hungry and sleepy.

He'd just made up his mind to return to the truck when he heard the sound of a treeing dog in the distance. It had to be Blue. Coon hunting was a nocturnal sport, and seeing as how it was the middle of the day, he was probably the only fool in these woods. Alvin's heart lightened, and he even forgot his gnawing hunger for the moment. Wanda would never have to know how close he came to losing his investment, and that was a good thing, because she could really be a bitch when she set her mind to it.

He stood still and quiet as he tried to get a bearing on the direction of the dog's barking. It wasn't easy, because the sound echoed off the hills and seemed to come at him from all directions at once. But Alvin was an experienced hunter, and he was used to honing in on the sound of his dogs at night. He finally decided on east and set off at a brisk pace. There wasn't much danger of the dog moving now that he had something treed, but Alvin wanted to get home. If he could eat and get in the bed within the next hour or so, he might be able to salvage the planned hunt tonight.

He came to a small stream, crossed it, and began to climb up a steep incline. He could have circled around the ridge, where the going was much easier, but it would have taken more time. Despite the fact that his was receiving a disability check for his back, Alvin could get around as well as anyone else, provided no one was watching. He didn't feel guilty about it; he'd put in his time in the mines, nearly sixteen years, and he figured he'd paid enough dues to be able to sit back and enjoy life. There would be no black lung disease for Alvin Hobbs, no sitting around and coughing up his lungs like he'd seen a lot of the old-timers do. That was bullshit. If the government was willing to pay him eighteen-hundred dollars a month because he'd been able to get his doctor to say his back was shot, so be it. He'd paid his taxes when he was working. He was simply getting his own money back from Uncle Sam.

He topped the ridge, breathing heavily, and stopped again to listen. The barking was closer now, and he could pinpoint its direction with little difficulty. Five minutes, maybe ten, and he would have his dog and be on his way. Blue wasn't likely to be loving life once Alvin got his hands on the mutt, but the dog had to learn. Alvin would be dipped in shit before he'd go through this after every hunt.

Suddenly, the dog let out a startled, shrill cry, and then fell silent. Alvin stopped, listening, but only silence greeted his ears. He called the dog's name, but received no response. This couldn't be good. What if a bear had snuck up on Blue while the dog's attention had been fixed on whatever he had treed? And here Alvin was, a five-shot .22 revolver and nothing else. His rifle was in the truck, but it was also a .22, no match for a bear. He had larger caliber guns at home, but that didn't do him a heck of a lot of good right now.

He considered turning back, then dismissed the idea. It could have been a copperhead, in which case he needed to get to Blue as soon as possible. If it was a snakebite, he could probably get the dog out of the woods and to the vet in time to save it. He hurried in the direction he'd been going, wanting to cover ground quickly but also mindful of his surroundings, just in case it *had* been a bear or some other predator.

The bright October sun created sharp, distinct shadows, and more than once Alvin thought he saw something pacing him from the corner of his eye, only to turn and see nothing but the shadows of the trees. He scolded himself. Now was not the time to get a full-blown case of the willies. True, he was alone in the woods, but it was the middle of the freaking day, for crying out loud. How many times had he been in these same woods at night? Hundreds, maybe more. Nothing had ever jumped out and grabbed him, and nothing was going to now.

Just the same, he took the revolver out of his pocket and carried it in his hand.

After five minutes of brisk walking, Alvin stopped to rest and get his bearings. Blue had to be close; he was sure he'd come in the right direction. He tried calling again, and again got no response. Alvin began to rethink the snakebite scenario. If Blue was simply hurt, and not dead, he would at least whimper, letting Alvin know where he was. The continued silence seemed to suggest that the dog was incapable of responding. Alvin had a sudden and powerful urge to make tracks back to his truck, but he brushed it aside. More than the simple fact of the money he'd be out if he lost Blue, he was curious—he couldn't just leave without finding out what had happened to the dog.

Something hit the ground near him. An acorn. Alvin looked up and saw movement in the trees above him. A squirrel, or possibly a bird. He gave another halfhearted call which garnered no response and started walking again. He was on edge. If Blue was dead, then something big must have gotten to him. He knew that most of the animals in the woods would not challenge a human, especially not in the broad daylight. A bear might, but only if was starving or had cubs nearby. Since it was fall instead of spring or early summer, there shouldn't be any young cubs around, and the abundance of food in the forest made starvation unlikely.

A thought hit him then, and he stopped. A mountain lion. He'd read somewhere that their numbers had been on the rise in recent years. A mountain lion would definitely attack a dog, and just might attack a human. But if a big cat had pounced on Blue, the dog would have fought back, even if he had been taken by surprise. Alvin had heard no sounds of a struggle, only a single, loud yelp, then nothing.

Something hit him on the shoulder and he nearly screamed. Another fucking acorn. Again, there was a rustling in the treetops, and Alvin, on impulse, aimed his gun into the tangled mass of branches and colorful, dying leaves, and squeezed off a shot. The squirrel, or whatever it was, did not come tumbling to the ground, but the ruckus in the treetops ceased.

Alvin sighed. He might as well head back home and face the music. At least he could tell Wanda that something had gotten Blue, instead of having to report that the dumb dog had simply run off. She would still be mad, sure, but she could hardly blame him for it, at least. As bad as he hated to, he would probably put off hunting tonight as well. He would be too tired. And, though he wouldn't admit it, the woods were still giving him the creeps, and he didn't think he wanted to return in the dark. Not tonight.

He turned and started back the way he'd come, and another acorn hit him, with force, this time in the back. He whirled around. The nut had not simply fallen from a tree—it had been thrown. An acorn falling straight down wouldn't have hit him where it did, and it wouldn't have stung like that, either. Someone was playing around with him.

"Who's there?" he called. No one answered. The thought occurred to him that one of his buddies might be screwing with him.

Maybe someone had come across Blue and realized that Alvin would be close by. They might be hiding now, laughing at him, petting Blue to keep him quiet.

No, that wasn't right. Alvin had heard the pain in the dog's yelp. None of his buddies would have done that to another man's hunting dog. If someone was out there, they must have taken care of Blue, and now they were after him. Alvin couldn't even begin to imagine who might do such a thing, but if the nut had not fallen from a tree...

He was hit again, this time on the cheekbone, just under his left eye. He cried out in pain and surprise, and brought the gun up, waving it wildly. Despite the fact that the acorn had hit him head-on, he hadn't been able to tell where it had come from. His eye began to water, blurring his vision.

"Don't think I won't put a bullet in you!" he yelled, and someone laughed. It sounded like a small child, shrill and high-pitched. What in the hell was a kid doing out in the middle of the woods? Alvin lowered his gun, not wanting to accidentally shoot some rugrat.

He was miles from anywhere. It was hard to conceive any set of circumstances which would have put a small child alone in the woods on Drover Mountain, but Alvin supposed anything was possible. Drug use was rampant in the area, especially oxycodone, which the media had labeled *hillbilly heroin*. The papers were full of stories about kids being taken away from their druggie parents. Alvin himself had never had any use for pills, preferring hard liquor when the mood hit him, but he knew what the drugs did to people. So he guessed that it was possible that a child had wandered off, unnoticed by strung-out parents, and ended up out here in the middle of nowhere. Not likely, but possible.

"Hey," he called. "It's okay. I'm not going to hurt you. Come on out where I can see you." He tried to keep his voice pleasant and non-threatening, but he ended up sounding like some creepy pedophile. He scanned the trees, looking for any sign of movement. From behind a large oak, a small head peeked out briefly, then disappeared.

"Gotcha," Alvin mumbled softly. He started toward the oak, walking slowly, not wanting to frighten the child. Maybe something good would come out of this messed-up day, after all. Surely someone was looking for the little monkey, and Alvin would be hailed as a hero when he came riding back into town with the kid in tow. Bob Lyle might be so impressed that he might look the other way the next time Alvin took a deer out of season or drove home from poker night with a bit of whiskey on his breath.

He reached the tree and stopped. There was an odor coming from somewhere; a foul, rotting smell that stung his nostrils. He looked around for the cause—a dead animal, maybe—but he didn't see anything.

"Don't be afraid," he said gently. "Nobody's gonna hurt you." There was no response from behind the tree, but Alvin heard a slight noise, like the kid had shifted around. The poor thing was probably scared shitless. Alvin supposed he would be, too, if their roles were reversed. He peeked around the trunk of the tree.

The kid was there, all right, cowering. It looked like a boy, but it had its back to Alvin, so he couldn't really tell. It was crouched on the ground in a kind of fetal position, with its head tucked down and its arms crossed over its knees. It was also buck naked, and its skin was caked with dirt and grime. Alvin realized that the awful smell was coming from the kid itself. He had a sudden, powerful burst of pity for the child, followed closely by utter contempt for the sorry excuse for parents who had let something like this happen to their kid.

"Hey there," he said softly. "It's okay. It's gonna be okay. I'm gonna get you out of..."

The child turned to look at him, and Alvin Hobbs screamed like a little baby. He dropped his gun and tried to back away, but his legs gave out and he dropped to his knees, his body convulsing with spasms of pure terror. There was nothing child-like about the thing's features; in fact, there was little human about them at all. It stared at him with large, black, bulbous eyes. There was no nose, only two holes set into the face which might have been nostrils. Its mouth was large and lipless, and the skin around it was pulled back to expose teeth like shards of broken glass. It hissed at Alvin.

He stared back at the thing, horrified but scarcely able to comprehend what he was seeing. He tried to scream again, but found that he couldn't; his throat felt totally closed off. He sensed movement around him and knew that others were approaching, but he was incapable of taking his eyes off of the thing before him. He was only remotely aware that he had pissed himself.

Something stung the back of his shoulder, and he realized that one of them was on him, its hideous mouth tearing through his jacket and into his flesh. His paralysis broke and he was up instantly, reaching awkwardly behind him as he tried to dislodge the creature from his back He grabbed something—an arm, maybe. The flesh felt leathery and dry.

Alvin took off at a sprint, and the thing on his back either fell or jumped off.

He ran, eyes wide, fists pumping in front of him. The day no longer seemed bright and sunny—shadows moved at his side as he ran, and the sunlight cast a wicked glare on the forest. From behind him came the guttural shrieks of his pursuers. He raced down the steep slope he'd ascended earlier and had almost made it to the stream when one of the creatures darted between his legs, became tangled there, and sent him sprawling to the forest floor. He jumped up, or tried to, but in an instant they were on him, weighing him down, ripping at his clothing. He felt teeth as sharp as razors ripping into his legs. For some reason, he thought of Wanda, and was sorry that he'd thought of her as being a bitch earlier. She was a good woman, really, and he loved her and knew that he would miss her.

He wondered if she would miss him.

Chapter One

"I'm not going back in there," Ron Seaver said, his expression stern. He was shaking his head for emphasis, and his lower lip jutted out defiantly. He looked like a little kid refusing to take a bath.

"Don't have much of a choice," Finn McCoy replied. "Not if you want to keep on breathing." He looked at Ron with no small amount of disdain. "If you shit in the devil's bed, he's likely to take notice of you."

"How was I supposed to know it was a demon?" Ron looked sick, his defiance beginning to melt away.

McCoy shook his head. Ron wasn't a bad guy, but he was a complete idiot. A self-proclaimed paranormal investigator, Ron spent his time hanging out in cemeteries and old, abandoned buildings, taking readings with his various instruments and snapping hundreds of photos of dust particles. He was harmless, for the most part, but this time he'd stepped in a pile of crap he couldn't scrape off his shoes. While performing a "cleansing" for a client, Ron had managed, through a series of mispronounced words in Latin, to royally piss off a major demon.

Now it was up to McCoy to minimize the damage. Getting the demon out of the client's house wouldn't be a problem, but ensuring that it wouldn't follow Ron home and fillet him like a rainbow trout might be a bit tricky. Demons were grudge-holders of the highest order, and once they got a whiff of your aura they could hunt you down anytime and anyplace they wished. To save Ron's mangy hide, McCoy would have to banish the demon, not just from the house, but from the physical world entirely.

"We went over this when I agreed to help," McCoy said. "I'll get rid of the entity, but the only way I can be sure that it works is if you're in there with me." In truth, Ron did not have to be there at all, but McCoy was intent on teaching the fool a lesson. For Ron's own good, of course.

"But it scratched me," Ron whimpered. He lifted his shirt to show McCoy, for the hundredth time, the small red welt on his side.

"It'll do a lot worse than that if we don't get rid of it."

"Couldn't you just do it by yourself? You know, one PI helping out another?"

"I'm not an investigator, Ron. I'm a handler."

"What's the difference?" Ron whined.

"Well, look at it this way. *You* investigated. Now *I've* got to handle it. And you're coming with me."

Ron looked miserable. He was scared to go back into the house, but he sure as hell didn't want the demon following him home. All of his electronic equipment and recorders would be of no help to him against the evil spirit. He had no choice but to do as McCoy said, like it or not.

"Okay," he said reluctantly.

"That's the spirit," McCoy said with a grin. "No pun intended."

They left the sidewalk where they'd been standing and walked up the front walkway to the house. It was a big colonial with a gambrel roof. McCoy thought that that the owner must be doing pretty well for himself, and wondered if Ron had charged for his services.

"The family isn't here?" McCoy asked.

"No. They ran out when the dining room chairs started flying around the room."

"Swell," McCoy said. He pushed the front door open and peered inside. Nothing seemed amiss, but McCoy was too seasoned to go waltzing in unprepared. He removed his canvas knapsack from his shoulder and set it on the front stoop. From within the bag he produced a small jar containing a powdery substance. He opened the jar, poured a small amount of the powder into his hand, and sprinkled it on himself. Then he turned and dusted Ron, who looked at him questioningly.

"Powdered lavender," McCoy said.

"Um, okay. Listen, Finn, I know you're really into this Voodoo stuff..."

"Hoodoo," McCoy corrected. "And I'm into whatever works, Ron. Now shut your trap and follow me."

McCoy stepped into the front foyer, Ron reluctantly on his heels. The air within the house was acrid—stale, with a bit of sulfur thrown in. The curtains had been drawn over each and every window, affording them limited visibility. The furnishings inside the home were modern, and in this room, at least, everything seemed meticulously neat and in order. McCoy flipped a light switch to no avail. He took a small flashlight from his knapsack and thumbed it on.

To their right, a doorway opened up into what appeared to be a den or sitting room. Directly opposite of that, to their left, was the dining room. McCoy headed in that direction, the beam of his flashlight sweeping the interior of the house in wide arcs. The house was silent except for a soft ticking noise, probably a large grandfather clock which McCoy had yet to see.

They stepped into the spacious dining area. Unlike the foyer, this room was a mess. The chairs that Ron had described as flying around the room now lay scattered on the floor, a few seemingly intact but most in pieces. The bulbs in the overhead lights had shattered, leaving shards of broken glass which crunched under their feet as they walked. The smell of sulfur was stronger here, and for the first time since entering the house, McCoy sensed a hint of the evil presence, but only for a split second, and then it was gone.

"We need to go upstairs," McCoy said, motioning at Ron to lead the way.

"But most of the activity happened here," Ron argued.

"I'm not debating that. The thing we're after, however, is upstairs."

"Why do I have to go first?"

"Because I've never been inside this house before, and you have," McCoy said impatiently. "Get me to the stairway, at least."

Ron backed out of the dining room and back into the foyer. He turned deeper into the house, past the sitting room. Just beyond that, to the right, was a staircase which led to the upper landing. McCoy went first, taking the steps slowly, one at a time. A cold draft drifted down the stairwell, causing their clothes to billow and turning their breath into a white mist. The temperature seemed to drop ten degrees for each step they ascended. By the time they reached the upper landing, Ron was visibly shivering.

They came out into a hallway which led to the four bedrooms and one bath on the second floor. All of the doors were closed, but Ron pointed out which doors led to which rooms. The door at the very end of the hall led to the bathroom. McCoy was less interested in that one; he sensed the evil presence in one of the bedrooms on the left side of the hallway.

"Stay close," he whispered, and moved to the first door on the right. The vibes here were bad, but just to be sure he went to the second door and stood in front of it. Satisfied, he returned to the first door. He turned and gave Ron a serious look.

"Okay, this is it. It's liable to get nasty from here on out, so I want you to stay behind me and keep out of the way. Got it?"

Ron nodded solemnly, but he looked ready to bolt at any minute.

McCoy grasped the doorknob. It felt nasty in his hand. Stifling his revulsion, he twisted the knob and eased the door open.

It was even darker in this room than in the rest of the house, though that shouldn't have been physically possible unless the windows had been boarded up. When dealing with demonic entities, however, the laws of physics went out the window. The smell of sulfur was nearly overpowering. As far as McCoy could see, nothing moved within the room, and no sounds crept out of the darkness.

He shifted the knapsack so its contents would be within easy reach and eased into the room. The décor indicated that it was a child's bedroom; a boy, from the looks of it. The small bed was made to resemble a racing car, and the bed covers were decorated with cartoon images from a popular children's movie. The curtains on the window were pulled back, but no light entered the room form the outside. Evil dwelt within the room, and McCoy could feel it watching him with cold, hate-filled eyes.

"Ostendo vestri," he said softly. *Show yourself*.

He received a menacing, otherworldly growl in response.

"Ostendo vestri!" McCoy called loudly, and Ron jumped backwards with a pitiful gasp. Behind the bed, in the corner of the room, the darkness began to deepen and solidify. The room grew colder by half, causing goosebumps to form on the flesh of McCoy's arms. The growling resumed, rising in intensity, like a maddened pit bull approaching at breakneck speed. A toy car raced across the floor and into a wall, the impact shattering it into a thousand pieces.

The demon formed from the shadows and regarded McCoy with unbridled hate. It had taken on a canine-like appearance, something between a dog and a wolf. It was a favorite among demonic entities, meant to inspire terror and dread. Looking at the thing, McCoy was forced to admit that it worked pretty damn well.

"Tell me your name," he said, this time in plain English. Now that the demon had been forced to reveal itself, the rules of communication were much more lax. More so than human spirits, dealings involving demons tended to rely heavily on structure and ritual. It irritated McCoy to no end, and he just wanted to be finished with the whole affair.

"You'd like that, wouldn't you?" the demon purred. Demons were gender-neutral, but could take on the appearance and characteristics of either male or female as they pleased.

"I demand it," McCoy said flatly.

The demon made no reply. Instead, it began to move toward them, its powerful haunches swaying with each step. With a shriek of undiluted horror, Ron turned tail and sprinted across the hall and down the steps, his screams echoing in the downstairs rooms and out the front door. McCoy gave his departure only passing attention; his eyes were fixed on the evil entity in front of him.

"You know you can't harm me," he said. His tone was casual but steady.

The thing stopped and looked at him, its head cocked the way a dog's might. It appeared to smile, inasmuch as its twisted features would allow.

"Do you think I wish that?" it asked.

"Of course. It's what all of your kind desires—the torment and suffering of humanity."

The demon laughed, its voice changing from that of a sultry young siren to that of an old, rattle-breathed hag. "Yes," it croaked. "You're right. But sometimes the deed is more pleasurable to watch than it is to perform."

McCoy paused. Demons often spoke in vague terms or riddles, and seldom answered any question with a direct response. Obviously, the entity was inferring that it need not harm McCoy because someone or something else was going to, thus saving it the trouble. Since demons, like ghosts, could see future events to a certain extent, he thought it might be prudent to pursue the conversation a little further.

"You can only watch it if it actually happens."

As if in response, the demon changed forms, no longer a mutated wolf-dog, but a young girl in a white sundress. The child had blonde hair and appeared to be about three or four years old.

"Do you recognize me, McCoy?" the demon-child asked in a little girl's singsong voice.

"No," McCoy answered, but he was suddenly on guard. He didn't know who the little girl was supposed to be, but he thought that he *had* seen her before, somewhere. It could have been a child he'd passed on the street or had glanced at in a park. She could have been anyone.

"Then mark my face," the child said with a giggle. "I am your doom. I am your destruction. All who stand in my way shall perish."

"Are you trying to kill me with riddles?" McCoy asked. He was no longer in such a hurry to banish this particular demon. Though they were notorious for being deceivers, it was possible that this one might have information that could be helpful, if not downright critical. But it was like trying to trace a phone call in an old movie—you had to keep the demon engaged long enough to find out what you wanted to know.

The child-thing giggled again, then its face mutated into a terrifying visage. The eyes were black as night and bulged from their sockets. The mouth stretched out and became a thin slash along the lower part of its face. The nose all but disappeared, leaving two gaping wound-like holes in its place.

McCoy had to force himself not to shrink away from this sight, for he knew the creature standing before him all too well. A Sluagh, one of the Unforgiven Dead. He suddenly felt very cold. Outside of Europe, he knew of only one place where the Sluagh could be found.

Shallow Springs.

"Ah, but you recognize me now!" the demon cackled, seeing McCoy's revulsion. "Your end is coming, Finn McCoy, and I will be there to bear witness!" With a deranged laugh, the demon spun and leapt back into the shadows in the corner of the bedroom. McCoy, too slow on the uptake, fished a bottle of holy water out of his knapsack, already knowing that it was too late. The demon was already fading, its laughter receding like the horn of a speeding train. By the time McCoy uncorked the bottle, it was gone. Sunlight poured into the room, and the temperature shot up a good thirty degrees in seconds.

"Shit," he said to the empty room. The cartoon characters on the bedspread grinned at him.

Ron was waiting safely across the street when McCoy came out of the house. He gave McCoy an apologetic look.

"Is it gone?" he asked.

"From the house."

"What?" Ron was suddenly alarmed, his embarrassment forgotten. "What about me?"

McCoy reached into his knapsack and retrieved the lavender powder. He tossed it to Ron.

"Your new bath powders," he said.

"But..."

"Relax, Ron. It wasn't there for you. It wanted to give me a message."

Ron looked unhappily at the jar, but remained silent. McCoy left him standing there and went to his truck. It was a beat-up relic with fading camouflage paint. It would never win a race, and simply making it to his destination was sometimes questionable, but he couldn't bring himself to part with it.

"Time to go home, Boo," he said, referring to the nickname he'd given the truck long ago. He patted it on the side of the bed. A few flakes of rust drifted to the ground.

McCoy removed his straw cowboy hat and ran a hand through his long, graying hair. He was tired—he tired a lot easier than he used to. He also suffered from insomnia, and his knees hurt like a bitch when it rained.

Aging really needed a better PR guy.

As he was pulling himself up into the seat, his cell phone rang. He looked to see who was calling and immediately had a bad feeling. Considering the events that had just taken place in the house, this couldn't be good. He hit the answer key and put the phone to his ear.

"We've got a problem, Finn," the voice said from the phone's speaker.

"We? You got a mouse in your pocket, Lyle?"

"Always the comedian. And after I've covered your ass so many times."

"Your ass more than mine, if I remember right."

Bob Lyle laughed. It was a nervous laugh. McCoy didn't like the sound of it.

"I've got seven people missing," Lyle said finally. "Two this week alone."

McCoy winced. "From the same area?"

"No. That's the problem. They're scattered. One from the Mill Dam, two from Drover Mountain. One near Miller's Ridge. The rest are even closer to town."

"Closer than usual?"

"Closer than ever before."

McCoy was silent. People were always disappearing in Shallow Springs. Usually, however, they vanished at a rate of one a year, maybe two. Sometimes they disappeared in groups, like the loggers and that environmentalist fellow a few years back, but that was rare. The Fey were hungry, but they were also sly and not prone to draw unwanted attention to themselves. Something was happening, something bad.

"You still there?" Lyle asked.

"Yeah. I suppose you want me to come up there."

"Who you gonna call?" Lyle meant it as a joke, but it failed miserably.

"When?"

"Today, if you can."

17

"Let's make it tomorrow," McCoy said. "Early, say nine or ten."

"I'll be at the station," Lyle said. Then he was gone.

McCoy stared at the phone, but it wasn't about to give him any answers. He sighed wearily. That town was going to be the death of him yet. He should have burned it to the ground fifteen years ago, when he'd left for the supposedly last time. The place was like a black hole, constantly drawing him back in.

Well, he wasn't going to worry about it until tomorrow. He'd messed things up enough for one day. Shallow Springs would wait.

The Fey would wait. Just as they had, for centuries now.

Chapter Two

It was late afternoon when McCoy arrived home. His small bungalow, out of place among the nicer homes which lined the street, was located near the dead-end of the road. Most of his neighbors were elderly couples, and the neighborhood was usually quiet. Unless it was mid-morning, when they all seemed determined to drown out the sound of each other's mower.

The grass in McCoy's yard was considerably higher than that of his neighbors. Lawn maintenance was not high on his list of priorities, ranking somewhere between cleaning the gutters and a trip to the dentist. Up until this summer, he had employed a teenager from the next block over to mow, but the little fart had up and gone off to college, leaving McCoy to fend for himself. He supposed he could work something out with one of the old guys on his street, but somehow it just seemed wrong to pay Grandpa to mow his yard for him.

He guessed he would have to break down and do it himself. It wasn't, after all, a large yard, and there were no ornamental trees or bushes to mow around. McCoy liked it that way. The fewer hiding places between him and his front door, the better. He kept the interior of the house the same way—sparsely furnished, nowhere to hide. It made things a lot easier for a man in his line of work. You never knew when something bad might follow you home, and a small, well-lit home with few furnishings was preferable to a large, dark, and cluttered one.

He left Boo sitting at the curb and went to the door. He carried only two keys on his keychain: one for the truck, the other for his front door. That way, if it was dark or if he was in a hurry, it was not difficult to locate the right key. He unlocked the door, glancing down at the red brick dust under the threshold as he did so. It didn't appear to have been disturbed. The dust was an old Hoodoo trick used to keep out unwanted spirits, and it worked without fail. But since there were other things besides spirits which would gladly strip him of his hide and use it for a throw rug, he also carried a 9mm pistol under his shirt.

McCoy went inside and shut and locked the door behind him. He removed the gun and placed it on the desk beside his computer. When doing research, he used the computer more often than not. When accuracy was critical, however, he turned to the two overstuffed bookcases which flanked the computer desk. He couldn't trust everything he read on the internet, but the books were far more reliable.

He wasn't interested in research at the moment. He wanted a beer. Ron had frustrated him; the demon had alarmed him. And the call from Sheriff Lyle had disturbed him to no small degree. On top of all that, he would soon be making his second trip to Shallow Springs in less than a year. When the fun got started, it just kept a-rollin'.

He went to the fridge, grabbed a beer and popped it open. He took a long swallow, relishing the coldness and taste. The back door in the kitchen led to a small porch, and he opened it and went outside. The rocking chair on the porch was his favorite seat in the house. He plopped down into it, removed his worn straw cowboy hat, and placed it on the small table beside the rocker.

There was a connection between the demon's warning and the call from Lyle; it would be foolish to think otherwise. The demon had taken the form of a Sluagh, and the only place within thousands of miles where a Sluagh could be found was the Springs. You didn't have to be a rocket scientist to see the connection.

The Sluagh might be responsible for one or two of the disappearances in the Springs, but McCoy couldn't fathom the creatures being behind all of them. More than likely, other members of the Fey were at work here, also.

Damned fairies.

The Fey, or fairykind, were more concentrated in Shallow Springs than anywhere else this side of the Atlantic. Contrary to popular belief, they were not cute little creatures that flitted about on butterfly wings. They were mean, nasty beings, and they despised humans and reveled in their suffering.

The Sluagh were possibly the nastiest of the lot. They were the Hosts of the Unforgiven Dead, vile creatures which housed the souls of the evil and unrepentant. They travelled in packs like wild dogs and were known to prey on small children and people travelling alone. They usually tore their adult victims to shreds, but the children were abducted, never to be seen again.

McCoy wondered about the child whose form the demon had taken. Had she been kidnapped by the Sluagh? For a moment there was almost something, a bit of a memory, but then it was gone. He shook his head. His powers of recall weren't what they used to be; age was, in truth, like a thief in the night. He was only forty-six, but he felt decades older. His body wasn't what it used to be, either. Some mornings, it was a struggle just to get out of bed.

He finished the beer and decided it had been good enough to warrant another. He'd made it halfway to the fridge when his cell rang. He took it out of his shirt pocket, handling it the way a bachelor might handle a shitty diaper. He really hoped it wasn't Lyle.

It wasn't. With a sigh of relief, he clicked the talk button.

"We still on for tonight?" asked Amanda Porter.

"You bet. Might have to make an early evening of it, though."

"Why? You got another date after me?" she teased.

"Tomorrow. Early. But he's a sight uglier than you, I promise."

"A client?"

"Bob Lyle, over in the Springs," McCoy said. Amanda said nothing, an indication that she didn't exactly approve. "Some people are missing," he went on. "May be something, may be nothing."

"Bullshit. We *are* talking about Shallow Springs."

"Yeah, well. Let's not talk about that now. We've got a Chinese buffet to terrorize."

"You're going to get yourself into trouble over there," Amanda pouted.

"Already did. I met you there, didn't I?"

"Not looking to score tonight?"

"Okay, okay. I'm shutting up. Be ready at six?" he asked.

"Yeah. But we're taking my car. I'm not riding in that deathtrap."

"Shhhh! Boo's really sensitive."

"I'm serious. My car."

"If you insist. See you in a few hours."

He hung up and checked the time. After four. Time to hit the shower and wash the smell of demon off. That, and the lavender powder. He shambled off to the bathroom, burying thoughts of Shallow Springs, determined to have a good evening.

***

Ben Rollins was bored. Sometimes when Ben was bored, he drank. Other times, he hopped into his '87 Camaro and went for a drive. He was currently doing both simultaneously, though he was only two beers into the drinking side of it. But that was all right. The sun was just starting to sink behind the mountains, and he had all night.

21

He was currently heading down Duncan Road, and there were two reasons for this: since he was drinking and driving, it was prudent to avoid the four-lane highway and stick to the more deserted back roads, and Duncan Road was chock full of curves, which his car handled expertly as he sped along.

An eighties metal band blared from the stereo system, which had cost roughly twice what the car had. The car was equipped with t-tops (the actual tops having long since disappeared) and Ben's long, blonde hair blew in the wind as he drove. He'd thought recently about having it cut—most of the guys he knew wore their hair short or completely shaved nowadays—but Connie liked it, and he wasn't quite tired of getting into her pants yet. Not that he was really serious or anything, though he suspected she was; she'd been dropping little hints here and there lately. But Ben Rollins was no woman's property, and sooner or later Connie would figure that out. Then she could either get used to the idea or take a hike. It really didn't matter much to Ben either way.

He hadn't passed another vehicle for quite some time, and he was beginning to get a little bolder with the curves. There hadn't been any rain for days, so there wasn't any danger of rounding a turn and finding a puddle of water in the road. Nor was there a likelihood of encountering the law this far out in the boonies. That was a good thing, because he was currently all out of favors from Sheriff Lyle.

Up until a month ago, Ben had held a job with the town's public works department. The job had been hard work with lousy pay, but it did offer a few fringe benefits, one of which being that Lyle and his cronies tended to look the other way as far as town employees were concerned. Up to a point, of course. You couldn't go out and kill somebody, but you could get away with a little drinking and driving, as long as you weren't too far over the limit. But Ben had shown up late for work one time too many, and that had been the end of that.

He finished his beer and threw the dead soldier out of the car and into the ditch. It shattered as it hit. He bent down to fish a fresh brew from the carton in the floorboard, uncapped it, and when he looked back up he saw the girl standing in the road.

With a curse, he locked the brakes and went into a skid. A lesser man would have surely crashed right then and there, but Ben could handle his car, and he managed to pull out of the skid without overcorrecting. He missed the girl with inches to spare and squealed to a stop a hundred feet or so down the road. Wide-eyed and breathing heavily, he looked down and saw that he hadn't spilled his beer. Thank God for small miracles.

Ben looked back at the girl. As far as he could tell, she had never even moved. But that wasn't the strangest thing. The light was getting dim, but Ben could swear that she was completely naked.

He put the car in reverse and eased back to where the girl stood. His eyes had not been deceiving him; she was a bare as the day she'd been born. She looked to be about eighteen or nineteen, though it was really hard to tell with girls these days. Her long, blonde hair was mussed up and hid most of her face. Of course, Ben wasn't exactly looking at her face. She was thin, but built like the proverbial brick shithouse, and he felt himself become aroused despite the near miss he'd just had.

"Hey," he said. "Are you all right?"

The girl said nothing, and did not turn to look at him.

"What the hell are you doing out here in the middle of the road, with no clothes? Jesus, I damn near ran you over!"

She turned then, and he saw that she was beautiful. Not good-looking, like Connie, or even really hot, like Dana Riley, but *beautiful*, like a model or movie star. He didn't recognize her, but that didn't surprise him. She was probably nine or ten years younger than he was, and he didn't run with a younger crowd.

She smiled. It was a lopsided, goofy smile, and her eyes seemed unfocused. It dawned on Ben that the girl was high on something. Of course she was; why else would she be standing in the middle of the road in the middle of nowhere, and buff naked to boot? Pills, probably. Ben himself did not snort anything, though he wasn't against the occasional joint. But he had seen plenty of people doped up, and this chick looked like she was trying to become their poster girl. It was sad, because she really was ultra-hot.

"Get in," he said. "I'll take you home. Or wherever." The thought of driving the girl to her parent's house in her present condition did not appeal to him. Most likely, he'd get shot before he could get out of their driveway.

The girl made no attempt to move, just stood there looking at Ben with that silly smile on her face. He couldn't leave her out here, but he couldn't take her home, either. Not yet, not until she came down off whatever mountain top she was presently on. The obvious answer was to take her back to his place. She could sober up there, and he could find something for her to wear from the stuff Connie had left lying around. Plus, he might get lucky if he played his cards right.

"Come on, hop in. I'll get you into some clothes." He gave her a sly wink. "I won't bite, I promise."

Her eyes focused somewhat, and her goofy smile transformed into a seductive pout. She stepped close enough to lean inside the car, putting her full breasts within inches of Ben's face. He didn't think he'd ever seen such a perfect pair, and he was suddenly obsessed with getting the girl back to his house.

She brushed her unruly hair away from her face. Ben tore his attention away from her boobs long enough to see that she had pale blue eyes and soft features. Her lips were full and dark, begging to be kissed. He suddenly realized he had never felt such desire for a woman before, and the feeling frightened him.

"You won't bite?" she asked. Her voice startled him into jumping, even though she spoke softly, almost a whisper. Her words seemed to have a hypnotic effect. He felt as if he were being suffocated by pleasure and lust.

"No," he managed. "I won't. Promise."

She smiled, her face a portrait of sexuality. But was there something else there, as well? A cruelty, lurking just below the surface? And maybe hunger, too? She leaned closer and put her mouth to his ear. He could feel her breath, hot and sultry. Her tongue brushed lightly against his neck, and he nearly melted with desire.

"I bite," she whispered with a flirtatious laugh. "We all bite out here."

"You do?" In some back corner of his brain, alarms were going off, but he couldn't bring himself to care.

"Uh-huh." Her voice was so freaking sexy. He needed air in a bad way, but he couldn't tear himself away.

The car shuddered slightly, like something had crawled onto the trunk. Then another something. The rational part of him, what was left of it, wanted to turn and look, but he couldn't tear his gaze away from the girl. He felt like he was going to explode at any second. More and more small bodies climbed onto the vehicle, and he could actually feel the car begin to squat from the added weight. But still he could not look away from her. His lust held him immobilized, aware but uncaring about anything but her.

"Do you want me?" she asked.

"Yes," he breathed.

"Forever?"

"Oh God, yes."

She held his eyes with hers; those pale, sexy, evil eyes. He saw a red droplet appear on her cheek, then another. He didn't understand at first, but then the pain suddenly hit him, hot as fire, and he felt his attackers upon him, biting and clawing and forcing him down. Still he could not tear his gaze away, even as his flesh was ripped and his blood sprayed onto the car's upholstery. He continued to stare at her after the life faded from his eyes.

Ben died without ever seeing what had killed him.

Chapter Three

"Have you noticed that there are other people here?" Amanda asked as McCoy returned with his third plate.

"Yeah," he said as he sat down at their table. "So?"

"I'm guessing a few of them came here to eat. If you leave anything, that is."

McCoy shrugged and took a bite from an eggroll. "I'm a growing boy," he mumbled. "Besides, banishing demons takes a lot out of a man."

"But you didn't actually banish it."

"Well, if you want to split hairs and get all technical..."

"And you're still going back to Shallow Springs. Even after the demon's warning."

"It wasn't exactly a warning. Demons are liars and deceivers. It was probably just trying to rattle me enough so it could escape."

"And you think it's just a coincidence that Lyle called right after that?"

"There is such a thing. That's why they came up with a word for it: *coincidence*."

Amanda rolled her eyes and took another sip of her drink. There was absolutely no arguing with Finn McCoy. It was like the old saying about trying to teach a pig to sing. But she was beginning to care for him, deeply, and she did not want him to go and get himself hurt. Or worse.

"Besides," he said, "I'm going in the daytime. I'll be back long before dark."

"Yeah. Think back about six months. That's what you thought when you came to my house on the lake."

"Well, there was no way I could have anticipated a water hound."

Last April, Amanda had come seeking McCoy's help because she thought something was stalking her. As it turned out, something *had* been stalking her, and it had damned near killed both of them. Since then, Amanda had moved into an apartment about three miles from McCoy's house, and had taken a job as a paralegal with a local law firm.

"Maybe I can take off tomorrow," Amanda said. "I want to come with you."

McCoy nearly choked on a bean sprout. "Forget it," he said. "We moved you out of that place for a reason. You've got no business going back."

"And you do?"

He gave her a look, his *honest* look, which meant that whatever he was about to say was serious, all joking aside.

"People are missing, Amanda. They're probably dead. It's been going on for years, but now it's really picking up for some reason. I need to find out why."

"But why you?" She was frustrated almost to the point of tears.

"Who else do these people have? Lyle? He's not going to risk his ass to help them."

"But he's willing to risk yours, and you're just dumb enough to let him."

He saw that she was worried, and he didn't want to cause her any pain. He had taken quite a shine to her in the last six months, and he also knew that she felt the same way. But this was what he did, this was what he *was*. Amanda knew that coming into it, and she would have to make peace with it sooner or later.

"I can't turn a blind eye anymore," he said. "Like I said, this has been going on for decades. Probably centuries. I could have done something before, but I didn't. I've been no better than Lyle, worrying about my own hide. But I can't do it anymore. It has to stop."

Amanda realized at that moment that she loved this man, and that epiphany caused her both joy and pain. On one hand, she was ecstatic to learn that she could still feel this way about a man after her first marriage had ended in an ugly divorce. But it also frightened her to fall for a man who battled ghosts, demons, and monsters on an almost daily basis. She wasn't sure if she could handle that pressure.

"Finn," she said. "I understand why you feel you need to do this. I really do. And I won't tag along tomorrow when you go to see Lyle. But you can't keep treating me like some fragile little girl. Not if you want this to work. I'm a grown woman, and I can handle myself."

"I never said that you couldn't."

"No, but you treat me that way. If it weren't for me, that water hound would have eaten you for supper, remember?"

"Yes."

"Okay then. I'm not asking to be your sidekick or anything, but you can't keep me locked out. I know what's out there now, and I worry about you."

He started to say something, thought about it, and took another bite of food instead. They sat in silence for a few minutes, and Amanda was beginning to worry that she'd jinxed it, that she should have kept her mouth shut. Finally, though, he looked up at her.

"It's hard for me," he said. "Aside from my parents and a few friends when I was young, I've never really been close to anyone. It's not that I didn't want to. I couldn't afford to. With all the things I've seen…I know it's selfish, but I've always been afraid of letting someone get close and then losing them."

His words touched her even more, and she had to fight to keep her eyes from misting up. Though she might be setting herself up for pain later on, she couldn't think of another man she'd rather be with.

"Okay," she said, trying to keep her voice steady. "Enough of this mushy stuff. What do you plan to do after Lyle fills you in?"

McCoy, genuinely relieved that the conversation was going in a different direction, shrugged. "If I have time, I'd like to visit a couple of the sites where someone went missing. See if I can find anything. We'll go from there, I guess."

Amanda didn't miss the *we'll* instead of *I'll*, and she smiled to herself. He was trying, God love him, and that was all that she could ask for.

"Do you think these Sluagh are responsible for the all missing people?" she asked.

"I don't see how they could be. They travel in packs, and they have a pack mentality. There's no definitive leadership, though. No alphas strong enough to dominate the others. They fight amongst themselves more often than not. When they attack, it's more of a crime of opportunity. They happen upon someone, or someone happens upon them."

"And you think whatever's going on now is more coordinated?"

"It seems to be," McCoy agreed. "Besides, the Sluagh tend to stick to the more isolated areas. I've never heard of them coming in close to town."

Amanda studied her empty plate. "What about the little girl? Are you sure you didn't recognize her? She has to fit into all of this somehow."

"Maybe, maybe not. Like I said, demons are deceivers. They like to mess with you. It's possible that the little girl has nothing at all to do with this. She may not even exist. Still…"

"What?"

McCoy shrugged. "Just for a second, I thought that maybe I had seen her before. A long time ago, perhaps." He started to pick up the remains of his eggroll, then decided against it and pushed his plate away. His appetite was gone. "At any rate, I don't see what she could have to do with anything, unless she's one of the recent disappearances."

"Well," Amanda said, "you'll find out tomorrow. You ready to blow this joint?"

"Yep. Wanna come back to my place for a nightcap?"

"Is that what they're calling it nowadays?"

"You can call it whatever you want," he said, flashing his best wolfish grin. "As long as you show up."

"Ah, Finn McCoy. You do have a way of charming the pants off a lady."

"Exactly my intention," McCoy smiled.

Their waitress, seeing that they had finished their meal, brought their check and two fortune cookies. Amanda tossed her cookie into her purse for later and went to get her car. McCoy took the check to the cashier and paid. While he was waiting for Amanda to bring the car around, he unwrapped his fortune cookie, broke it open, and popped the cookie in his mouth. Absently, he unfolded the small piece of paper with the message on it. He glanced at it, did a double take, and reread the message again.

Soon everything will make perfect sense.

Amanda arrived with the car and McCoy hopped in, wishing fervently that fortune cookies would be a little more damned specific.

***

Bob Lyle was in a foul mood. Lately, he stayed in a foul mood, and that fact served only to piss him off even more. Lyle had held the position of sheriff for more than two decades, and during that time he had come to the conclusion that ninety percent of the people in Meade County were idiots. Out of the remaining ten percent, at least nine percent more were *slobbering* idiots. That left one percent (of which he counted himself one) who had more brains than God gave a mule.

Whatever brains Ben Rollins had possessed were now scattered about the interior of his car. Judging from the looks of it, and from what Lyle knew of the man, the sheriff felt justified grouping Rollins into the slobbering idiot category. The loser hadn't even been able to keep a job with the town crew, and that was saying something. The mess in the car was merely a product of natural selection. Thinning the herd, so to speak.

The problem was that Lyle's herd was being thinned at an alarming rate recently. This tended to make the rest of the herd extremely skittish, and a skittish herd wasn't likely to re-elect its shepherd. Lyle had been sheriff for so long that he wasn't sure if he could do anything else, and he wasn't in any hurry to find out.

Lyle looked up from the gory mess inside the car and saw two of his deputies emerge from the woods beyond the edge of the roadway, each carrying a flashlight. The smaller one, Paul Kenner, was a little rat of a man who definitely fell into the ninety percent. Personally, Lyle wouldn't trust the man to guard a pile of rocks, but Kenner's uncle was on the town council.

The big one, John Talbot, was a good guy. Lyle actually liked John, and that was saying a lot because Lyle hardly liked anyone at all. Big John was a good deputy. He was serious about his job and followed orders well. Best of all, Big John knew when to keep his trap shut. That was a valuable commodity in the world of law enforcement. Sadly, it was also a commodity in very short supply among Lyle's deputies.

"Find any more of him?" asked Lyle.

Big John shook his head. "Nothing. No blood, no pieces of clothing. Wherever the rest of him is, it isn't here."

Lyle had figured as much, but he was still disappointed. He had hoped beyond hope that this wouldn't be connected to the others, but he should have known better. Something had set those damn fairies on a rampage, and now his only hope of controlling the situation was Finn McCoy, the King of the Slobbering Idiots. Lyle disliked McCoy with a passion. The man was reckless and cocky, two attributes Lyle despised in a person. McCoy was also the luckiest son of a bitch ever to walk the face of the Earth, by Lyle's estimation. By rights, something should have had the fool's ass on a platter years ago. But McCoy was blessed; he could fall in a tub of shit and come out smelling like a rose.

"You want us to look around some more?" Kenner asked.

"No. I do not want you to look around some more. I want you to get someone out here to clean this mess up. And be quick about it. When word gets out we'll be up to our armpits in rubbernecks driving by here to see what's up."

"Sure thing, Chief." Kenner hurried to his cruiser to radio dispatch. Lyle watched the moron go with open contempt. He hoped to God Carl Kenner lost his seat on the council come next election.

"So, what do you think?" Big John asked when Kenner was safely out of earshot.

Lyle rubbed at his forehead. "I don't know. Some wild animal, I guess. Maybe a bear or mountain lion."

Big John's look told Lyle that he knew he was being fed a bunch of bullshit, but he was professional enough not to call the sheriff on it. There were very few people in Shallow Springs who knew the whole story. McCoy knew more than anyone, Lyle guessed, but so far he'd had enough common sense to keep fairly quiet about it. Besides, most people viewed McCoy as a kook—eccentric but harmless. And though most of them liked him, they weren't likely to listen if he started running off at the mouth about killer fairies.

"People are starting to get scared," Big John said. "Bunch of people missing, and now this. I know how you feel about calling in the state boys, but..."

"We're not calling anyone, least of all those idiots."

"But..."

"But nothing, John. We handle this in-house. There's no evidence here of anything other than an animal attack. As for the others, some of them will probably turn up. Even if some of them don't, it's not that unusual for this area. People turn up missing all the time. Most of it's probably tied to drugs."

"How could we tie Bessie Peterson to a drug deal gone bad?" Big John asked. "The woman is seventy-four and plays the organ in church every Sunday."

"She's also on every medication known to mankind," Lyle said gruffly. "For all we know, somebody whacked her and made off with her pills. It happens every day."

Big John had no answer for that, so he said nothing more. Lyle turned his attention back to the car. In the darkness, even with the flashing blue lights illuminating it, it didn't look all that bad. But looks were deceiving. It *was* that bad; the whole situation was bad. And now that even Big John was beginning to question Lyle, the window of opportunity to put a lid on this thing was starting to close.

As bad as Lyle hated to admit it, everything now hinged on McCoy. Lyle was not about to go fairy hunting, and he couldn't very well send his men without telling them what they were looking for. Not only would he land himself in a rubber room, but on the off chance that someone believed him, he would face numerous questions concerning cover-ups and blatant misdirection of certain past events. He could not answer those questions without ensuring the sudden and final end to his career as a law enforcement officer. He might also go to jail, and Lyle would rather face the Queen Fairy herself than to be put behind bars.

So, once again, he found himself in the position of having to kiss Finn McCoy's ass. As unpleasant as that thought was, it sure beat the aforementioned alternatives. As much as Lyle would like to see McCoy fail, or even better, get eaten by some big, hairy monster, McCoy's success was the only way Lyle would make it through this unscathed. He would be polite. He would offer McCoy whatever limited assistance he could. Then he would sit back and let McCoy do his thing, whatever that might be, and hope that everything worked out to his advantage in the end.

It was getting late, and Lyle was tired. It was going to be a long night. McCoy would be arriving in the morning, and Lyle would be able to pass the buck. Until then, he had a few matters to take care of, the first being to ensure that the little rat Kenner would keep his mouth shut about what he'd seen here. There wasn't much to tell, really, but it would be best to keep everything close to the vest until the whole matter was resolved.

Lyle spat at Ben Rollins' blood-soaked car, motioned for Big John to follow, and walked over to talk to the rat.

Chapter Four

The drive to Shallow Springs wasn't as pleasant as the one McCoy had taken six months prior. Instead of a bright spring day, he now faced a dreary October morning. A cold drizzle forced him to keep Boo's wipers arcing noisily across the windshield.

He wanted to find out what was going on, but he wasn't looking forward to seeing Bob Lyle. The sheriff was usually pleasant enough, but McCoy could see through the man's false front. He knew that Lyle couldn't stand him, and the only time the sheriff had anything to do with him was when there was a problem with the Fey.

Lyle had been re-elected consistently over the past twenty years, despite the fact that the only person that he actually cared about was Bob Lyle. Or, to be more specific, Bob Lyle's career. He had covered up more deaths and disappearances than the CIA. Due to the tireless efforts of the sheriff, the citizens of Shallow Springs were blissfully unaware that they shared their town with monsters.

It would have done no good for McCoy to have tried to enlighten them. Just as he was aware of Lyle's true feelings about him, he knew that people considered him to be a flake at best and a carnival sideshow freak at worst. He was okay with this, mostly because he didn't give a shit what people thought of him, but also because it allowed him to enjoy his privacy. Having no close friends allowed him to spend his time as he pleased, and there was no one he felt he had to take care of.

At least there hadn't been before Amanda. McCoy hadn't expected to fall in love with her, but it had happened anyway. He had been quite the womanizer before they had met and had assumed those habits would continue until he died in his sleep or something nasty got him.

But Amanda was different. She was intelligent. She was strong. And she was sexy as hell. When she'd found out the truth about the Fey and other creatures that lurk in the night, it had shaken her to her core, but she had refused to succumb to fear. She had accepted and adapted. McCoy had never before seen anyone deal with that knowledge as well as Amanda had, and she had gained his instant respect.

He had not, however, foreseen that she might want to become involved in his work, and he was not sure how to handle this unhappy development. He cared too much for her to risk seeing her get hurt, but he risked alienating her if he shut her out completely from his work. It seemed to be a no-win situation.

It was a little after nine when he passed the town limits sign. Returning to Shallow Springs was always bittersweet; he had been born and raised in the town, and he had also barely escaped it with his life. That had been fifteen years ago, and he could probably count on one hand the times he'd been back since. Lately, he'd felt increasingly guilty over that fact. He was likely the only one who had a chance in hell of helping the people of the town, and he had all but turned his back on them. Like Bob Lyle, he had been more worried about his own skin than stopping the loss of innocent life.

His last trip to the Springs, when he'd come to help Amanda, had marked a change in him. While battling a water hound, an ancient Celtic monster associated with the Fey, he had become increasingly resentful of the fairies for the torture they had inflicted on him and the people of the town. A burning rage had been ignited within him, and he was determined to somehow end the Fey's reign of terror.

To do this, though, he would have to find the portal. They Fey were extra-dimensional beings, not from this dimension but able to exist here as they pleased. Travel back and forth, however, required a portal, similar to the ones demons used to materialize in this reality. Obviously, there was a portal located in or around Shallow Springs, but McCoy had never been able to locate it.

The rain began in earnest as he pulled in front of the sheriff's office. A streak of lightning lit up the gray and swollen sky, followed closely by a window-rattling clap of thunder. If the weather didn't break soon, it would be useless to stick around after meeting with Lyle.

McCoy hopped out of the truck and ran to the front door, getting thoroughly soaked in the process. He opened the door and went into the front lobby. His wet shoes squeaked as he walked across the tiled floor. A female deputy sat behind the front desk, and McCoy struggled to remember her name. Debbie? Diane? No. Deidre. He was pretty sure that was it. He walked over to the desk and stood there dripping and smiling.

The deputy glanced up at him, was apparently not impressed, and went back to whatever she was doing on her computer. McCoy stood there a moment longer, and when she failed to look up again, he cleared his throat. With an annoyed expression, she looked at him again, eyebrows arched.

"Deidre, is it?" he asked, and her expression softened just a little. Apparently she was mildly impressed that he had remembered her name. It was a start, anyway.

"Yes, Mr. McCoy. How can I help you?"

"Got an appointment with the sheriff. Is he in?"

Deidre picked up the phone, hit a button, and informed Lyle that McCoy was waiting. After a brief pause, she hung up the phone and motioned McCoy towards the sheriff's office. He tipped his hat and smiled. Deidre snorted and returned to work.

McCoy stopped at the sheriff's door and knocked. He might as well be on his best behavior; he was going to have to work with Lyle, like it or not.

"Come in," the sheriff's voice boomed from the other side of the door.

McCoy opened the door and stepped inside. As a token of respect, he removed his hat. He was pleased to see the gesture wasn't lost on Lyle.

"Finn," the sheriff said, rising from his desk. "Long time, no see." He offered his hand and the two men shook.

"Yeah. Don't make it up this way too often." said McCoy.

"Well, it's good to see you, anyway." Lyle was laying it on thick. McCoy figured the situation was even worse than he'd thought. "Sorry it has to be under these circumstances. Have a seat."

McCoy sat down in one of the chairs which faced the sheriff's desk. He glanced around the office. Lyle was an avid fisherman, and the walls of his office were decorated with angling memorabilia and several stuffed fish. There was even one of the plastic fish that moved and sang a song when you pushed a button. McCoy imagined Lyle, alone in his office, pushing that button repeatedly and grinning as the fish sang.

"So what's the score?" McCoy asked.

Lyle sighed. "One more than when we talked yesterday. Kid named Ben Rollins. We found his car out on Duncan Road last night. Most of his innards were still in it."

McCoy was surprised. "That's eight in all. When did the first one go missing?"

"Two months ago, give or take."

"Damn. That's averaging two a week. They've never been this bold before."

"Not by half," Lyle agreed.

Though he dreaded it, McCoy asked, "Anybody I know?"

35

Lyle shrugged. "First was Evert Adams. He went ginseng hunting on Miller's Ridge and never came back home. Next was Bessie Peterson. They must've taken her out of her house. The place was a wreck. After that was Dennis Yates."

"I know Dennis," McCoy said. "Drives a tow truck for Green's Towing."

"He did. Went out on a call around ten at night. We found the truck in a ditch the next day."

"Where was that?"

"Just the other side of the Mill Dam. Barb Hutchins went two days later, about a two miles out of town on 719."

McCoy was mentally mapping the locations, and he was starting to see a pattern.

"It was quiet for almost a week, then Harv Stanley went out on Wednesday for his poker night with the boys. Found his car on Monster Road the next morning."

"The next one was near Drover Mountain too, wasn't it?"

Lyle seemed impressed. "Yep. Alvin Hobbs was coon hunting there. Never made it back."

"Okay," McCoy said. "You said the Rollins fella bought it on Duncan Road. If the pattern I'm seeing holds, the seventh one was somewhere around Cane Creek Road."

"You win the kewpie doll. Missy Newton left for work Tuesday morning. She works—or worked—at the hospital. She never made it there."

"You see the pattern?" McCoy asked.

Lyle nodded. "They started on Miller's Ridge, came down the mountain to the dam, came close to town, then headed across Drover Mountain and down Monster Road. From there, they crossed Cane Creek and ended up on Duncan Road."

"They? Do you have any idea which ones we're talking about?"

"Not exactly," Lyle shook his head. "Of course, I don't know 'em like you do. We found some tracks, though. There were a lot of 'em, and they were small buggers."

McCoy winced. He hadn't believed that the Sluagh could be responsible for all of the disappearances, but the evidence was sure pointing that way. But if it were the Sluagh, then there was something else curious about the whole thing.

"No kids," he mumbled.

"Excuse me?"

"I was just saying that none of the victims were children."

"Thank God," Lyle said.

"Yeah. I mean, it's a good thing that no kids were taken, but it's also a bit puzzling."

"Why's that?"

"If it's the Sluagh that're doing this—and it sounds like they are—then the fact that no children have been taken just doesn't fit. The only thing the slaugh enjoy more than ripping a person apart is kidnapping a child. They go out of their way for that sort of thing."

"Maybe the opportunity hasn't presented itself," Lyle offered.

"Maybe," McCoy nodded absently. He sensed there was more to this than met the eye.

"So you're saying if a child were present, it would be the primary target for these things?"

"From everything I know about them, yes."

"Damn fairies. That's all I need." As if things weren't bad enough, now Lyle had to worry about a kid being taken. That would drive a stake through the heart of his re-election bid for sure. These things had to be stopped, and fast. If that meant throwing McCoy a little more assistance than the sheriff had originally planned, so be it.

"I'm assuming these things can be killed."

"Oh. Yeah." McCoy had been lost in thought. "The Sluagh are the Hosts of the Unforgiven Dead. They're more or less human souls trapped in Fey bodies. An iron stake or knife will work, among other things."

"Wait. You said *human* souls?"

McCoy nodded. "As the legend goes, they are either lost souls or souls so evil that they have no place in either heaven or hell. Of course, they've become so twisted that you wouldn't recognize them, even if you had known the person well in life."

Lyle snorted with disgust. He disliked all this supernatural mumbo-jumbo. He'd dealt with it firsthand, and so he was forced to believe in it, but that didn't mean he had to like it. He folded his hands on his desk and looked down at them.

"Let's get to the bone here, Finn. Outside of me and you, nobody in this town knows what's really going on. I think a few people suspect it's something more than random vanishings or crime-related disappearances, but I seriously doubt anyone's considered fairy abduction. So I'm limited in what kind of assistance I can offer. I can give you manpower for searches, but I'm damn sure not going to tell my deputies to be on the lookout for goblins or trolls. You can use whatever resources I have, as long as you run it by me first."

McCoy considered this. Lyle had never before been so generous with offers to help, and that meant the sheriff was desperate. It was tempting to take Lyle up on it, but the thing that really stuck in McCoy's craw was that the sheriff was only out to save his job. He wasn't worried about the people who were being slaughtered, not really. He knew that Lyle considered himself superior to the citizens he was sworn to protect, and it left a bad taste in McCoy's mouth.

Still, things might start to get rough, so it wouldn't be prudent to dismiss the sheriff's offer out of hand. McCoy needed to use tact, which was scary, because it was something he had little experience with.

"I appreciate it, Bob. I really do. Tell you what, though. Let me do a little checking around first. You know, under the radar. When I get a better idea of what we're dealing with, I'll fill you in and we can go from there."

Lyle nodded. He looked relieved. "We've got to move quickly, Finn," he said. "Before anyone else gets hurt."

Like you care, McCoy thought, but he gave Lyle a look of grim determination and nodded back.

***

Thankfully, the storm had passed by the time McCoy left Lyle's office. The sun was trying to peek out from behind the broken clouds as he opened Boo's door and climbed into the cab. He put the key in the ignition and started to crank it, then reconsidered and sat back in the seat. Through the drying windshield, he could see Main Street. Now that the rain had stopped, people were back on the sidewalks as they busied themselves with the day's errands.

From where he sat, he could see Gravely's Hardware. McCoy realized he hadn't set foot in that store for over fifteen years, yet it was still there. And, by the looks of it, still doing a thriving business. Farther up the street was the Blue Moon Diner, where he'd once had the audacity to ask Audrey Marshall for a kiss. How old had he been? Fourteen, maybe? He tried to remember but couldn't. Beside the diner was the old arcade, put out of business years ago by the release of home gaming systems.

A wave of nostalgia passed over him, mixed with a good healthy dose of guilt. Why had it taken him so long to come back, to try to help? Sure, he'd returned on the rare occasion over the years, but it was never more than a quick foray in and out, and only when the matter was urgent. He had been more than willing to push Shallow Springs to the back of his mind, storing it there like a chest of unwanted junk.

But maybe he was missing the important question: why did he want to help now? What had changed in the past year that made him want to take on ridding the town of the Fey as his personal quest? God knew he had been perfectly content to just avoid the fairies for years. There had to be a reason.

He thought that maybe there were two reasons. The first was Amanda. She was a good, strong person. When he compared himself to her, he found himself lacking. That had never mattered to him before, simply because he hadn't cared for anyone deeply enough to value what they thought of him. But that had changed. Amanda was the type of person who would have the courage to do the right thing. McCoy wanted to be like that, too.

Secondly, he was getting older. He no longer held any illusions of immortality. And if death were to find him, he wanted to be doing something worthwhile.

Something *right*.

He twisted the key and started the truck. Though it might prove to be the end of him, he had decided that it was time to take the fight to the Fey.

Chapter Five

She stood on the rocky crag and watched the man. She was well above him, out of earshot, and he had no idea she was there. He couldn't see her; she was too far off and she took care to keep hidden from his eyes.

She couldn't recall how many times she had watched the man's passing. Hundreds, at least. Maybe more. He came every day, no matter the weather. Sometimes it was earlier in the day, sometimes later, but always he came, travelling the same well-worn path, always alone.

She never allowed the others to come with her when she watched the man, and she took great care to make sure that she wasn't followed. If the others discovered the man, they would want to rip him up, and though they usually did as she told them, there was always the chance that she might lose control. It was hard enough to keep them from the children, but she had promised them a nearly unlimited supply of adults to prey upon, and so far that had satisfied them.

Except for the man in the woods below her, she didn't care about any of the other grown-ups in the town. In fact, it pleased her to watch the others stalk and take their prey. The people were useless bags of bones and meat. They lied. They made promises they had no intentions of keeping. They cheated on each other and rejoiced in one another's suffering. They deserved to die.

On the path below, the man stopped. He stood still, and he seemed to be listening intently. She instinctively crouched and held her breath, even though it was impossible that he could have seen or heard her. He stood for a moment longer and then resumed walking. As she watched him go, a feeling of sadness crept over her. She found herself wondering how long he would go on. He was getting older, and one day he would simply be unable to continue. But he was determined, and he would go on for as long as he could.

That thought both comforted her and saddened her even more.

She turned from the man and headed back across the rocky hill. Sharp rocks dug at her bare feet, but they had been toughened by years of never seeing a shoe. It would be dark soon and the others would be getting restless. It would not do to leave them unsupervised for much longer.

They would be waiting for their Queen.

She strode through the shadows, already smelling the blood and hearing the screams.

***

McCoy pulled the truck onto the earthen shoulder of Duncan Road and glanced up at the sky. The clouds had mostly dissipated, and judging from the position of the sun, he had two, maybe three hours before it would be time to head back. Despite his newfound resolve, he had no intention of remaining in Shallow Springs after sunset. Besides, he had promised Amanda, and she would be furious if he went back on his word.

A recently-burnt road flair signaled that he was at the scene of last night's festivities. This was the spot where Lyle and his boys had found Ben Rollins' car, ready- decorated with parts of Ben himself. McCoy wasn't exactly sure what he was looking for, but he wanted to look, anyway.

He got out, made sure Boo was pulled far enough off the road, and began to walk slowly around the area. There was a lingering sensation, like an aftertaste, that something bad had been there, but it was weak and fading. A few splotches of dried blood stained the pavement, unnoticeable to anyone unless they were looking for it.

McCoy walked into the roadway. There were fresh skid marks on the pavement; it looked as though someone had swerved to avoid hitting something in the road. He looked closely but could not discern what that something might have been. He pulled his cell from his pocket, saw that he had just enough signal to make a call, and dialed Lyle's number. The sheriff picked up on the second ring.

"Did you find anything in the road last night?" McCoy asked.

"Besides the car? No."

"Nothing blocking the way, something he would have had to stop for?"

Lyle paused. He could see where McCoy was going with this.

"No. Just the car," he said finally.

"Then why did he stop, Bob? He didn't pull off the road. He stopped *in* the road. The Sluagh are small, like children. But they don't look like children. If I'd seen them in the way, I would have plowed through them and kept on truckin'."

"Maybe it was dark. Maybe he thought they *were* kids."

"Maybe," McCoy agreed, but he was unconvinced. "Thanks, Bob. We'll talk later."

"Okay. Be careful out there."

McCoy stuck his tongue out at the phone and hung up.

It didn't make sense. If Rollins had come upon a group of Sluagh, he would have recognized them as not being human, and it was unlikely that he would have stopped. Even if it had been dark, and he *had* stopped, it was doubtful that the creatures could have overwhelmed him before he had a chance to get moving again.

He followed the skid marks. They went on for nearly a hundred feet, then stopped. *Here* was where Rollins had come screeching to a stop. And if that were the case, and the car was found back where Boo was parked, then Rollins must have backed up.

Why would he have done that?

Because he'd backed up to look at whatever had been in the road, that's why.

It hadn't been a rock or a tree: the Sluagh wouldn't have bothered to move it, and Lyle and company would have found it when they arrived. It was possible that it had been an animal, perhaps a cow, but animals are sensitive to the Fey and it wasn't likely a cow had been standing in the road while the Sluagh were hiding nearby.

He realized that he was coming up with more questions than answers. In fact, there were no answers at all, just a lonely, deserted stretch of two-lane road.

He walked back to Boo, certain that he would find nothing more here. He had time to check out one more location before packing it in for the day. Cane Creek Road was the closest, but McCoy wanted to visit Drover Mountain while he still had some light left. If he were going to see anything, it would probably be on that desolate pile of rock and dirt.

He turned back toward town, took the first left, and crossed Cane Creek Road. Monster Road lay before him, and Boo shuddered, as if dreading the steep, twisting drive. Freshly-fallen leaves covered the blacktop, which was already damp from the recent rain. McCoy wished for better tires as he started up the mountain.

This had never been one of his favorite places, and he had avoided it when he'd lived in the Springs. Much like Clairbourne Lake on the other end of the county, it consistently gave off bad vibes. As a youngster, even though he had the ability to see and sense the Fey and other paranormal entities, he had not been afraid of the town or most of its surrounding area. The lake and the mountain were two exceptions.

Very few people still resided on Drover mountain. The timber companies had bought up much of the land, and had acquired timber rights to the land they couldn't buy. The town did not furnish water and sewer services to this area, and the cable TV company flatly refused to go past the foot of the mountain. Add to this the harsh driving conditions in the winter, and it made the mountain unattractive as a home site to all but the most diehard back-to-nature nuts. Even most of those had moved to greener pastures after that bad business with the loggers several years back.

If McCoy had been able to forget about the creatures that lurked in the hills, he might have been able to enjoy the natural beauty of the mountain itself. As it was, he could no more enjoy looking at the autumn scenery than he could sucking on a dog turd. Each and every tree, though breathtaking with their colorful, changing leaves, was liable to harbor a tree spirit, or dryad. Trolls resided in the shallow caves and under rocky outcrops. Fir Darrig, or shape shifters, dwelt in the hollowed-out trunks of dead trees.

It would seem a small wonder that any person could walk through these woods without suffering a horrible death, but the Fey were nothing if not cunning, and they were experts at not drawing unwanted attention. For this reason, most people would be relatively safe trampling about the forest in the daytime, even if they travelled alone. Traversing the mountain in the dark would be much trickier, but there were very few people who would attempt that in the first place.

Since the Fey were known for their sly constraint, it was a mystery to McCoy as to why the Sluagh had suddenly gone on a killing spree. It certainly did not benefit the Fey as a whole, because more deaths and disappearances meant more attention and scrutiny. Indeed, if he and Lyle were not successful in their efforts to stem the tide, the area would be crawling with state police, and possibly the feds, in no time at all.

McCoy entered a section of switchback curves that slowed his progress to a crawl. He glanced out of the side window repeatedly, hoping to catch a glimpse of something, but nothing moved in the woods except an occasional bird or squirrel. He couldn't be sure where Alvin Hobbs had been when he had met his end, but he knew where Harv Stanley's house was, so he could make an educated guess as to the general area from which he had vanished.

McCoy rounded a steep curve which was followed by a short straightaway. There was movement in the woods to his right, and a girl, naked as a jaybird, exploded into the roadway. She stopped and stared at McCoy, her eyes wide with surprise. Then she darted into the trees on the opposite side of the road.

The whole thing was over before McCoy even thought to hit his brakes. He sat there for a moment, dumbfounded, then wheeled Boo to the shoulder. He put the truck in park and jumped out. The girl had been moving fast, and she had entered the forest several yards up and to his left. He grabbed his 9mm and took off in pursuit.

Small branches slapped at him as he ran. He thought he caught a glimpse of the girl, far ahead, but she seemed to be outdistancing him at an impossible rate. He realized that he couldn't hope to catch up to her. His best bet was to slow down and follow her tracks. Presumably, she had to tire of running at some point.

McCoy slowed to a walk. He was wheezing and gasping for breath, and this from sprinting maybe fifty or sixty yards. He was really out of shape; he could no longer deny the fact. Twenty years ago, he may have given the girl a run for her money, but now...

The surrounding woods were unnaturally quiet. No startled birds flew noisily into the treetops, which would have given the girl's position away. McCoy circled over to the approximate path the girl had taken, and was surprised by the lack of prints or broken vegetation. It seemed impossible that she had been able to run so swiftly through the woods without disturbing the forest floor.

On an even more puzzling note, he did not sense the presence of any Fey nearby, and he had not sensed anything when the girl had run out in front of him. This by itself did not mean much, for his senses were far from foolproof, especially when he was not alert for danger. But his gut feeling told him that she was not Fey. If that were the case, what was she doing out here? And why the stripper act? It was not overly warm due to the cloud cover and rain earlier.

He walked around for a few more minutes, but he knew it was a lost cause. If he had time, he might luck upon her trail, but it would be getting dark in a few hours. In the dark, he was likely to walk into an ambush, and that would be the end of it before he could even get started.

Reluctantly, he headed back to the truck. He was sure the girl hadn't been running from anything; she didn't have the look of someone being pursued. And she hadn't meant to be seen. She had looked genuinely surprised when she'd seen McCoy in the road. So, either she was on some mighty fine drugs or she was a part of what was going on. McCoy was willing to bet the farm it was the latter.

It just kept getting more confusing. As far as he knew, the Fey had never associated with a human, much less conspired with one. Especially not a hot, naked chick like the one he'd just seen. McCoy was suddenly sure that this was more than a group of Sluagh going on a random killing spree. Something else was at work here, something that he should be seeing but was unable to.

He reached the truck and was about to get in when his cell rang. The sound startled him, because he hadn't thought he could get a signal there. But then he remembered reading about a tower being placed somewhere on the mountain. He looked down and saw that his bars were maxed out. He pushed the talk button.

"Hey, sexy," Amanda said. "Not up there chasing women, are you?"

McCoy opened his mouth to reply, thought about it, and remained silent.

"Are you there?"

"Yeah. Almost dropped my phone. Where are you?"

"On my way home from work," she said. "Not all of us have trust funds to live off of. Are you still in Shallow Springs?"

"For the moment. I'm getting ready to head back. Things are screwy up here. I need to sit back and try to wrap my head around it."

"So you don't want any company tonight?"

"To the contrary, my dear. I need someone to bounce ideas off of."

"They're calling it that now?"

"Seriously," he said. "I've managed to dig up a lot more questions than answers."

"Well, I need to jump in the shower. I could come over in a couple of hours if you'll be back by then."

"I will be."

"I can stop and get chicken?"

"That'd be great. See you in a little while."

"Finn?"

"Yeah?"

"Be careful."

"Every chance I get."

McCoy ended the call, then immediately hit the talk button again. He needed to make a call while he had a good signal.

"What's the word?" Lyle asked when he answered.

"I'm up on the mountain now, but I'm getting ready to head home. Thought I'd let you know."

"Did you find anything?"

"Maybe. Listen, it might be a good idea to put some patrols around here tonight. And out Duncan Road, too."

"Okay. I can do that."

"And tell your boys to use extreme caution if they come up on a beautiful, naked girl."

"What?" the sheriff asked. "What in the hell are you talking about?"

"I think I know why Ben Rollins stopped in the middle of that road."

Chapter Six

It was nearly eight when McCoy arrived home. Amanda, ever a poster girl for punctuality, pulled in right behind him. He hopped out of Boo and went to open her door.

"Impeccable timing," he said as she got out. He bent over and gave her a kiss. It felt like winning the lottery.

"Keep that up, and you'll be bouncing the mattress instead of ideas," she said. She shoved a bucket of chicken at him. "I didn't get drinks."

"There's beer and soda in the fridge."

They went inside. Amanda set out the food while McCoy went to the bathroom. It had been a long drive back from the Springs, and he was pretty sure he'd soon be able to add prostate trouble to his growing list of ailments. Hooray for getting old.

"So, did you find anything interesting?" Amanda asked when he rejoined her at the kitchen table.

"Plenty," he replied as he sat down. "I just don't know what to make of it. There's definitely something funny going on in Shallow Springs."

"There's an oxymoron," she said. "Funny and Shallow Springs don't exactly go together."

"Fine. *Weird*."

"That's better."

"Lyle's got his back to the wall, and he knows it. I don't think these killings are just going to stop on their own. In fact, this may just be the beginning."

"Is it the Sluagh, like you thought?"

McCoy shook his head. "I'm almost positive it is. But something's different. They've never been so bold or organized before. And I saw this naked girl.."

"Whoa. Time out." Amanda had been about to take a bite of chicken, but she let it fall back into her plate. "You didn't think to mention that when I called?"

"Oh, I thought plenty. Then I came to my senses."

Amanda flicked a piece of biscuit at him. It bounced off his nose.

"Okay," he said. "Here's what happened. I was driving up Monster Road, and this girl comes busting out of the woods, not a stitch of clothes on. She stops for a second, looks at me, and then takes off. I tried going after her, but it was no use."

"See? I knew you were up there chasing women."

"Well, I didn't have a prayer of catching this one, believe me."

"Do you think she was one of them?" Amanda asked.

"No. I mean, I'm pretty sure she was human."

"Maybe she was being chased."

McCoy shook his head. "She was going somewhere. In a hurry. She didn't expect to see anyone on the road. It surprised her as much as it did me."

"Are we talking young girl?"

"Nineteen, twenty. Somewhere around that. She looked...almost *feral*. I tell you, it was a sight to see."

"I bet it was," Amanda said with a smirk. "Do you think she's the same one?"

"Same as what?" McCoy asked, shoving a spoonful of mashed potatoes into his mouth.

"The little girl that the demon showed you."

McCoy froze, spoon still in his mouth. He looked like he'd just been told he was eating puréed ass.

"I swear, Finn. For being a big-time paranormal handler, you have the hardest time putting two and two together."

"Damn!" he said through the mouthful of potatoes. He swallowed. "It could have been her. I didn't get a good look at her face, but the hair color was right." He looked at Amanda. "How did I ever make it before I met you?"

"Just keep asking yourself that," she said with a smug smile. "And wipe your mouth. You've got potatoes dripping from your chin."

He took a napkin and ran it across his mouth. It made sense. He had almost forgotten about the image of the little girl. She had to fit into this somehow, and since she wasn't one of the victims...

"We need to find out who she is," he said. "She might end up being the key to this whole thing."

"And how do we do that?"

"We can try the internet, but it may not be much help. Maybe you could go with me tomorrow and research back issues of the local paper. Could be she's a local that's been reported missing."

It was Amanda's turn to stop in mid bite. "You want me to come with you?"

"Sure, if you can take off from work. But I want you to stay in town."

She looked at him, undecided.

"Meet me halfway on this?" he asked.

Amanda smiled. "Okay. I'm sure they can do without me for one day."

"Great. I want to get an early start. Can you be here around seven?"

"That depends on what time you let me go home," she teased.

McCoy thought about it.

"Let's make it eight," he said.

***

Big John Talbot had a quandary on his hands.

John was currently patrolling Duncan Road, on the lookout for who-the-hell- knew-what, but his thoughts were a thousand miles away. He knew he should be paying attention to the task at hand, but there were some hard questions nagging at him, and he just couldn't shut them out.

He had never wanted to be anything other than a cop. When he'd been a kid, he had never wanted to be a firefighter or astronaut. In high school, when other kids had been talking about college or trade schools, John had kept his sights set steadfastly on the Academy. At sixteen, however, he'd lost the middle finger of his right hand in an accident, and his dreams of the Police Academy had gone down the drain.

He had found renewed hope when Bob Lyle had hired him on as a deputy. Some people viewed it as only a step above a rent-a-cop, but to John, the job was a godsend. He even had aspirations of running for sheriff when Lyle decided to pack it in, hence the moral dilemma he was now facing.

On one hand, he was Lyle's deputy, and it was his job to support the sheriff and follow orders without question. This was something that John usually had no trouble with, but in the past few weeks, it had become increasingly difficult.

Sheriff Lyle had never been in the habit of explaining his orders or the reasons behind them, but since the disappearances had started, he had become downright closemouthed and openly hostile to anyone who questioned him. Normally, this wouldn't have overly concerned

John. Lyle could be a moody person, and when he was in a bad mood it was wise to avoid him as much as possible. But John saw something lurking behind the sheriff's unusually gruff disposition: fear. Something about this whole affair was spooking Lyle, and badly.

Then there was the sheriff's insistence that there be no outside help. This puzzled John most of all. Even an isolated town like Shallow Springs was hardly cut off from the rest of the world. News travelled quickly via the internet and cell phones. There was no way in hell they would be able to keep a lid on this for much longer. It made more sense to contact the state police before the state police contacted them, wanting to know what was going on because someone read something on one of the social media sites.

The final straw, as far as John was concerned, was that Lyle was hiding something from them. It was as obvious as the nose on the sheriff's face. If Lyle knew something and was keeping it purposefully hidden, then there was a chance that this whole thing might blow up on him. And if that happened, not only would Lyle go down in flames, but his whole department would go with him. John's dream of one day becoming sheriff would die as quickly as his dream of the Academy had.

Big John couldn't allow that to happen. He needed to find out what it was the sheriff was hiding, and once he had that information, he would have to decide which path he should take. If it looked like Lyle might be able to control the situation, he would go on being the obedient, faithful deputy he had always been. If it turned out Lyle was in over his head, well...then there might be a call made to the state boys, after all. John considered himself as trustworthy as the next fellow, probably more so, but he was also no fool. He knew that there was nobody to look out for Big John except Big John.

The cruiser's headlights cut a bright arc into the desolate night. John was moving slowly. He was in no particular hurry; Lyle wanted him patrolling the area until three AM, at which time Jeff Thacker would show up to relieve him. It was going to be a long night. There was no traffic. Most of the other deputies would have pulled over and grabbed forty winks, but John, his mutinous thoughts notwithstanding, was a good cop and took the safety of the public seriously.

He thought he saw movement at the edge of the dark woods to his left, and he stopped the cruiser and activated his spotlight. The tree line was suddenly awash with a brilliant light. Though there was no wind, some of the lowest tree branches swayed as if they had been recently disturbed.

"Somebody there?" John called in his most authoritative voice.

No answer came from the trees.

John put the car in park and hit the blue lights. He got out of the cruiser, hand resting on his firearm, and studied the woods. He started to walk closer to the edge of the road, thought about it, and reached back into the cruiser. He pulled his riot gun from its retaining clip, checked to make sure it was loaded, and then began to move cautiously toward the shoulder of the road. Whatever it was that had Lyle on edge had infected him, and he was suddenly unwilling to take any unnecessary chances. John was a big guy, but he had seen the mess at the scenes of the abductions. He wasn't about to end up a blood splatter on the pavement.

"I want you to move slowly out of the woods," he said. "Towards me. And I want to see your hands."

There was a faint rustle, then something that sounded like a hushed conversation. John tensed and leveled the shotgun at the sound. He couldn't be sure, but it had sounded like a woman's voice. He realized that he had not radioed in when he'd stopped, a flagrant breach of protocol, and he silently cursed himself.

"I need you to move slowly into the light," he ordered, but his voice now carried less authority than apprehension. He had messed up badly. He should have at least told dispatch his position, and probably should have called for some backup, given recent events. He could still call in, but he would have to back to the car, a move that could be perceived as fear or weakness.

He decided to risk it. There was no doubt in his mind that someone was out there in the dark, and since they had not responded to his commands, it was likely that they were up to no good. He began to back slowly toward the cruiser, keeping his eyes glued to the woods in front of him. The sound of his shoes scuffing against the pavement sounded much louder than it should have.

"Help me," a female voice drifted from the forest. It had come from just beyond the reach of the light. John stopped and listened. The woman had sounded weak, hurt.

"Ma'am? Are you injured?" he called.

"Help. It...it hurts," came the reply.

The voice sounded faint and pained, but Big John knew that if it walked like a duck and talked like a duck, it probably was a duck. And this was probably a trap. He resumed his slow retreat toward the cruiser.

"Just stay put," he said, trying to keep his voice steady and even. "I'm going to call in and get an ambulance out here." *And a bunch more cops*, he thought. He was within a few feet of the car when something bolted from the woods. It was small, like a child, but it was coming at him incredibly fast. If he had stopped to think about it, he probably wouldn't have pulled the trigger. But he acted reflexively, and the shotgun discharged with a deafening roar. His attacker was spun around by the impact. The thing gave an ear-splitting shriek and fell twitching to the pavement.

John looked at the thing. It appeared to be some sort of grossly deformed child. It's features were grotesque, though whether or not that was a result of the shotgun blast, he couldn't tell. It didn't appear to be bleeding, but its skin was smoking from the heat of the pellets. Incredibly, it seemed to be shaking off the effects of the gunshot.

"The hell?" Big John said softly. He instinctively knew that he had discovered something Lyle already knew, that this thing was part of the truth the sheriff was hiding. The thing was fearsome- looking, for sure, but it was relatively small. John had a hard time believing that this creature had attacked and killed eight grown adults, most of them men.

There was a shrill cry from the woods, and suddenly dozens of the creatures came bursting from the darkness. John did not even consider firing again. He turned and dove into the cruiser, shoving the shotgun in ahead of him. He was able to pull the door closed just as several small bodies slammed into the car with enough force to rock it. Though terrified, he retained enough sense to realize he had no chance of surviving if he stayed and fought. He jerked the cruiser into gear and stomped the gas. His left rear tire rolled over one of the things, and it emitted an unearthly howl as it writhed on the roadway.

John glanced into his side mirror and was horrified to see that one of the things had latched onto the rear door handle and was doggedly hanging on. His window was down, and he had the dreadful notion that the creature was going to climb its way up the side of the car and jump inside. Steering with his left hand, he grabbed the shotgun with his right and thrust it clumsily out the window. He was turned awkwardly in the seat, and the car began to veer between the narrow lanes. He aimed as best he could through the side mirror.

The thing saw what was coming, but the cruiser was moving fast and it didn't seem to want to relinquish its death grip on the handle. John squeezed the trigger, and the creature was blown away with a quickly fading scream. He tore the hell out of the side of the car as well, but was lucky enough not to puncture his tire, at least. The gun's report set his ears to ringing.

John spent the next several minutes nervously checking each of his mirrors to make sure nothing else was hitching a ride with him. After several miles, he began to calm down. The first order of business was to get back to civilization, somewhere with bright lights and other people. Then he would have to decide what he was going to do. He was going to have to make a call, but whether it would be to Lyle or the state police, he didn't yet know.

He sped toward Shallow Springs, thinking the town to be a safe haven.

***

She was furious.

It had finally happened. They had missed one, and a policeman, to boot. He would come back with many more, and now they would know exactly what to look for. And all because one of them had been overly anxious.

She had been afraid of this. There had been signs over the past several days that her control was starting to weaken slightly. The others were troublesome things, bitter and always fighting amongst themselves, and now that their bloodlust was growing, it was getting even worse. This was why she only brought twenty or so with her each time. Deep down, though she was their Queen, she was afraid that she wouldn't be able to handle the whole horde.

But now her hand had been forced. There would be no more time to pick them off one by one. Now she must rejoin the horde and somehow hold them together for one final march.

By dawn, they would bring the town of Shallow Springs to its knees.

Chapter Seven

McCoy lay in his bed and wondered if his luck might finally be turning around.

He glanced over at Amanda, who was snoring gently beside him. After dinner, they had decided that she should sleep over so they could get an early start in the morning. She had gone back to her place, packed a few things, and returned a short time later. As far as sleepovers went, this was a first, and they had both been a little nervous. The evening, however, had flowed at such a natural pace that they might as well have been living together for years.

He was as happy as he could ever remember being, but he was also scared. This was unchartered territory for him, and he was afraid he might do something to mess it all up. And then there was his job, or his life, or whatever you wanted to call it. He was scared that she might get hurt. He was also afraid that she might tire of looking into the darkness with him.

McCoy knew that he was not giving Amanda enough credit by thinking this way. She was one of the strongest and smartest people he had ever met. A lot smarter than McCoy himself, apparently. He had been so busy patting himself on the back for figuring out the girl's role in the disappearances that he had overlooked the connection between the girl he'd seen and the image the demon had taken. And he had a feeling that it might be an important, if not critical, piece of the puzzle.

He knew that he was missing something. He hoped that things might make more sense in the morning when they went back to Shallow Springs. Maybe Amanda might find something useful in the newspaper archives.

He didn't want to disturb her, but he had to pee. He was convinced that his bladder was shrinking by half every year. At the rate he was falling apart, he probably didn't need to worry about the Fey or demons or anything else getting him. He would simply whittle away to nothing.

McCoy crept out of the bed as quietly as he could and padded to the bathroom. He lifted the toilet seat and made a mental note to put it back down when he was finished. It was nice to think that he might have to get used to doing that.

When he finished his business, he tiptoed back into the bedroom. He was about to crawl back under the covers when he heard something. He froze and listened. It came again—a buzzing sound, something like a pissed-off bumble bee might make. He looked around but saw nothing. It sounded like it was coming from beneath the bed. He squatted slowly, ready for something horrible to erupt from the darkness, and realized that it was coming from his shirt, which he had discarded on the floor earlier. His cell phone was in the pocket of the shirt. He had set the phone to vibrate earlier in the evening.

McCoy snatched the phone from the pocket and trotted into the kitchen; he didn't want to disturb Amanda. He looked at the phone's display, but didn't recognize the number. With a bad feeling, he answered.

"McCoy."

"Finn McCoy?" came the deep voice, which McCoy couldn't place.

"That's right. Who is this?"

"My name's John Talbot, Mr. McCoy. I'm a deputy with the Meade County Sheriff's Department."

McCoy was able to put a face to the voice. "Yeah. You're the big guy. I've seen you around, but we've never been introduced."

"Yes, sir." Talbot sounded every bit the cop. McCoy wondered whether or not this was an official call. "I got your number from Deidre Pratt at the office. I hope you don't mind me calling so late."

"No. That's fine. Has something happened in the Springs?"

"You might say that." There was a pause, as if Talbot were unsure how to continue. Or if he should. "I saw something tonight, Mr. McCoy," he said finally.

"Call me Finn. Please. What was it that you saw, John?"

"I don't know. I mean, I got a good look at it and all, but I still couldn't tell you what the hell it was."

"Let me guess. It was about three feet tall and looked like the ugliest kid you'd ever laid eyes on."

"How'd you know that?" Talbot sounded shocked.

"It was either that or a really hot naked chick," McCoy said. "I figured you wouldn't be calling me in the middle of the night about her."

"Naked chick?" Talbot was confused.

"Never mind. I take it Lyle hasn't given you guys many details about what's going on."

Another pause, this one not quite as long. "No sir, he hasn't. I need to ask you a few things, Finn, but first, I need for you to understand something. I've always done my best to be a good cop."

"I'm sure you have," McCoy said.

"I thought long and hard before making this call," Talbot said. "I struggled with it. It's not in my nature to go behind my boss' back. But I've come to believe that the situation is more serious than he's led us to believe."

"You hit that nail on the head."

"Sheriff Lyle is dead set against calling in the state boys. I'm...not so sure. Do you think he's making the right call?"

It was McCoy's turn to pause. He knew very well Lyle's reason for wanting to keep the outside help outside, and it had nothing to do with the safety of the citizens of Shallow Springs. Be that as it may, McCoy had always gone along with it because he had a better chance of dealing with the Fey without the interference that the state police or feds would have provided.

"For the time being," he said, "it's a good call. You've probably heard that I was in town today. I met with the sheriff, and we came up with a game plan. I'll be back first thing in the morning, and I'm going to try to put an end to this before anyone else gets hurt."

"Yeah, I heard you were some kind of ghost talker. Do you think you can do it? The truth."

"I think I can, yeah. I've had experience with things like you saw earlier."

"What the hell was it?" Talbot asked.

McCoy sighed. "Well, John, now that you're in the loop, so to speak, you're going to need to be filled in on a lot of things. That's something best done in person, and it would be better if Lyle didn't know. We can meet up tomorrow, if you want."

Talbot considered this. "Okay. But just so you know, if anyone else turns up missing, I'm going to make that call."

"Fair enough."

"What time are you...what the..." Talbot broke off.

"John? Are you still there?"

Talbot did not reply. McCoy could hear what sounded like footsteps and low, heavy breathing.

"John, what's going on?"

"I just saw one of them," came the whispered reply.

"What? Where are you?"

"In the middle of town. It ran into the alley between the hair salon and the drugstore."

"Town?" McCoy was at a loss. None of the Fey had ever been so brazen before. If the Sluagh were actually in the town itself...

"McCoy?"

"Yeah."

"Still think you can stop them?"

"I hope so."

"Then you'd better get your ass over here. Right now."

The call ended.

***

"I'm going," Amanda said. "Just like we'd planned."

"That was before little nasty uglies started showing up on Main Street," McCoy argued.

"All the more reason I need to go. Do you think Lyle is going to have your back on this?"

"I can watch my own back."

"Yeah. Like you did with the water hound?"

"Are you ever going to let me live that down?" McCoy shook his head in exasperation.

"Probably not." Amanda finished tying her shoe and grabbed her jacket. "Are you ready?"

McCoy was beaten, and he knew it. He didn't have time to argue. If the Sluagh were slinking around in the town proper, it was only a matter of time before something really bad happened. If they dallied much longer, there might not be a town left by the time they arrived.

"Okay. But you stick to me like glue, got it?"

"Your own shadow won't be able to get between us."

"Good. Grab my knapsack. I'll get the guns."

McCoy carried two shotguns loaded with iron slugs. He also had a walking stick made from black rowan, which he had used to kill the water hound at Amanda's lake house. Black rowan was also called fairy wood, and it could hurt the Fey like no normal wood could.

He insisted on taking Boo, citing the possible need of its four wheel-drive capabilities. Amanda, though not happy, relented, and they loaded up the truck. It was nearly two AM when they left McCoy's house; driving at the truck's top speed, they couldn't hope to make the trip in less than an hour.

McCoy wasn't overly concerned about obeying the speed limit, but he didn't want to drive recklessly, either. There was little traffic at this time of night, and the weather and road conditions were good, but he still slowed when he saw the occasional pair of headlights approaching from the opposite direction. He didn't want to get pulled over by the cops. A quick call to Lyle would probably get him out of a ticket, but he couldn't afford the delay.

"Shouldn't you call ahead to Lyle?" Amanda asked as they sped through the darkness. "He may not even know what's going on."

"I've been debating that," McCoy answered. "I'd think Talbot would have already alerted him. If not, and I call, I'm going to have to explain why I was on the phone with one of his deputies, and that's going to cause tension between all of us. If things are about to get bad, we won't be able to afford the distraction."

"How bad will things get?"

McCoy shrugged. "I have no idea, to be honest. None of the Fey have ever had the balls to show up in the middle of town. Talbot said he'd seen one. Hopefully, it was just a scout. Even that would be bad, but at least it would be better than a whole pack of them."

"And if it is a whole pack?" Amanda asked. "How is word of this not going to get out"?

"It probably will, at least for as long as it takes for the government to get involved. Then it's anybody's guess. My bet would be they'd quarantine the area while they attempted to deal with the Fey. Afterwards, people who saw anything at all would be reconditioned, or else they'd just disappear."

"The government would do that?" Amanda sounded unconvinced.

"You have no idea."

"Yeah, and I probably don't want to. It's enough that I already know about ghosts and ghoulies and evil fairies."

"Yes, it is," McCoy agreed.

They grew silent, each lost in their own thoughts as they drove through the night.

***

The Sluagh stood at the base of the cell tower, looking up into the night sky toward the top of the structure. The tower stood at over two hundred feet, but the agile creatures had no fear of heights, for even falling from the top, though it might be painful, could not kill them.

There were a dozen of them, and they had a single objective: to inflict as much damage on the tower's delicate antennae array as possible. Through their Queen, they had learned that, by disabling the tower's equipment, they would ensure that the raid on the town would not be hindered by outside forces. How the Queen knew this, they did not know, and it was not their concern. She often went out alone to watch the humans and gather information. She was intelligent, and she knew the ways of the humans.

Miles away, another group was poised to take down the telephone lines which ran into the town. This, the Queen had assured them, would totally isolate the people of the town from the outside world. When the siege began, they would not be able to call upon other humans for aid.

Soon, they would have their run over the town. The only demand that the Queen had made was that the children were not to be touched. While this ran contradictory to the nature of the Sluagh, it was an acceptable arrangement due to the sheer number of victims that would be available. Also, a successful assault on the town itself would assure that the Sluagh would attain the dominant rank in the hierarchy of the Fey.

The Sluagh checked the position of the stars. It was time.

They began to ascend the tower.

Chapter Eight

Moonlight glistened off the old-style barber pole which hung above the entrance of Tyler's Barber Shop. A few doors down, a gentle breeze stirred the colorful flag which hung outside Kustom Krafts. The flag depicted a seasonal theme: fat, orange pumpkins and crisp, fallen leaves. Across the street, the display window of Elaine's Discount featured a plethora of Halloween decorations and costumes.

John Talbot was crouched low behind a cotoneaster hedge which formed the borders of Veteran's Park. The small park was situated on the northeast corner of the town square, and it offered John an unobstructed view of much of Main Street in either direction. For the last half hour, all had been still and quiet.

John took his cell phone from his shirt pocket and hit the speed dial. After a few rings, Lyle answered.

"What's it look like?" the sheriff asked.

"Nothing since the one I saw earlier," John replied. While he had recounted the account of his encounter on Duncan Road, he hadn't spoken to Lyle of his conversation with Finn McCoy. "Maybe it was a one-time deal."

"Don't bet on it, son," Lyle said. "Just keep your eyes peeled and let me know if anything moves. I've got men set up all over town, just so you know you're not alone out there."

"Yes, sir."

"Good man. We'll get through this, John. I'll get some help in here come daylight. Just sit tight, and..."

John looked at his phone. The display read *call lost*. He checked his signal strength. No bars. That couldn't be right. There was always a good signal here in town.

He caught a furtive movement from the corner of his eye and turned to look across the street. Something darted into the shadows between two buildings, but he didn't get a clear look at whatever it was. It could have been a dog. He tried to tell himself that.

John really hoped that Finn McCoy was on his way.

***

McCoy took the exit into Shallow Springs a little faster than he should have, causing Amanda to take a sharp breath and grab the truck's dash in an effort to steady herself.

"We won't be much help if we're dead," she reminded him for what had to be the tenth time since they'd set out.

"Sorry. The steering's not as tight as it used to be"

"The only thing holding this truck together is your stubborn love for it."

"Then there's a lot to be said for stubborn love."

Amanda had no argument for that, but she was too nervous and excited to sit still and remain silent. She pulled out her phone to check the time and noticed something strange.

"That's weird. I don't remember any dead zones right through here," she remarked.

"What do you mean?" McCoy asked.

"I don't have any signal. I could've sworn it was always maxed out through here."

McCoy slowed and dug his phone out of his pocket. He checked for a signal. Nothing.

"Maybe something's wrong with the tower," Amanda said.

"Well, if it is, it's probably no accident."

"The Fey, you mean?"

"The Sluagh, to be more specific. It just doesn't make sense, though. They've never been this coordinated in their actions. Someone or something has to be leading them."

"Do you think it's the girl?"

"I think she has something to do with it. I'm just not sure what. I'm positive she's not Fey, but I don't see how a human could get in with the Sluagh without getting butchered, much less manage to become their leader."

"Not even a theory?" Amanda asked.

McCoy shot her a glance. "Yeah, I've got a theory, but it would bend the rules of everything I know about the Sluagh, if not totally break them."

"I'm all ears."

"Okay, here goes. It's possible the Sluagh kidnapped her when she was a young child. I think most of the abducted children are sent back through the portal, to wherever it is the Fey call home. I don't know what happens to them once they get there, and I don't think I want to. But for some reason, this child stayed behind and was actually assimilated into the Sluagh horde."

Amanda wrinkled her nose as she considered the fate that befell those unlucky children. She also had no idea what had awaited them on the other side of the portal, but she was willing to bet money that death would have been preferable.

"As the child grew," McCoy continued, "she would have started to dwarf the other members of the horde. Also, though the Slough are intelligent, she probably would have begun to outshine them in that area, too."

"And her soul wouldn't have been corrupted like those of the Sluagh."

"There's that, too. You catch on quick."

"I've got a good teacher."

They topped a hill and the lights of town came into view. McCoy slowed considerably, not wanting to run blindly into a felled tree or other trap set by the Sluagh. The road, however, was clear, and soon they turned onto Main Street. The town looked deserted, but that was to be expected at such an early hour. The town housed no factories or large businesses, and it was too early for the coal miners to be changing shifts.

"I've never seen the town at this hour," Amanda said. "It looks creepy."

"In this case, looks probably aren't deceiving," McCoy commented. "Let's head for Lyle's office and hope he's there."

"Let's do. On both counts."

McCoy pulled up to the traffic light at the town square. The light was red. He started to pull on through; there was no other traffic, and who was going to give him a ticket, anyway? But something caught his eye over near the park. That something was John Talbot, who was presently trying to hide his massive frame behind a short, skinny hedge. He wasn't doing a very good job of it.

Talbot saw that McCoy had spotted him. He stood and motioned them over. McCoy wheeled Boo to the curb, and Talbot came up to the driver's side window.

"Jeez. I'm glad you came," the deputy said.

"Don't mention it. I'd already seen all the infomercials on TV, anyway."

"I might have spotted a couple more since we talked, but it's hard to tell. They're so damn quick." His expression turned sheepish. "Maybe I'm just being paranoid."

"You're not. They're here. I can feel them."

Talbot looked at McCoy to see if he was being bullshitted, and decided he wasn't. Then he looked past McCoy and noticed Amanda.

"This is Amanda Porter," McCoy said. "She's...with me."

"Ma'am," Talbot said, dipping his head. Amanda smiled in return.

"Have you brought Lyle up to speed?" McCoy asked.

"Yeah. As far as those ugly critters go, anyhow. I didn't mention our conversation."

"That's good. We don't need to be second-guessing each other. By the way, is your cell phone working?"

"No. I lost signal about ten minutes ago."

"That's what I was afraid of," McCoy said. "What about the radios in your cars?"

"We can talk around town to each other, but something must have happened to the repeater on Drover Mountain. Without that, we can't talk to anyone more than five or six miles away."

"Landline phones?"

"Out."

"And you still think you're being paranoid?"

"No," Talbot shook his head. "I guess not. But it'll be daylight in another three hours or so. If they were going to make a move, wouldn't they have done it by now?"

As if on cue, there was a gunshot from somewhere nearby, followed by a man's scream. Talbot drew his firearm, and McCoy grabbed one of the shotguns. They listened, trying to determine from which direction the sound had come.

"Sounded like it was a block over," Talbot whispered. "Cherokee Street, maybe."

"Are there other deputies out here?" McCoy asked.

"Yeah, but I don't know who's where. Lyle is supposed to be coordinating everything."

"Then we need to get to Lyle, and he needs to pull everyone back in. Alone, everyone out here's a sitting duck. We need to band together in groups."

"I'll hop in the back." Talbot practically stepped over the side of the bed and squatted in the back. McCoy pulled out and headed for the sheriff's office, his eyes scanning the shadows between the buildings. More than once he caught the scent of something, like a faint odor on the wind, but it was gone quickly.

They travelled the two blocks to the station without incident. McCoy pulled directly in front of the building, where the area was well-lit. Motioning for Amanda to stay in the truck, McCoy got out and jogged around to her side. Sensing the coast was clear, he opened her door and helped her out. Talbot hopped out of the bed, and they grabbed their things and went inside.

There was no one at the front desk. McCoy called out and received no answer. He looked questioningly at Talbot.

"I'll go check Lyle's office," the deputy said. He walked down the hall and was gone for less than a minute before reappearing. He shook his head. "Doesn't seem to be anyone here."

"Was Lyle here when you last talked to him?" McCoy asked.

"I don't know. I called his cell. I just assumed he was here."

From somewhere outside, there was another burst of gunfire.

"Yeah, well we'd better find him, and fast," McCoy said. "Where's the radio?"

"Dispatch operates from that desk." Talbot pointed to a desk near the back wall. There was a base radio sitting on it.

"Go see if you can contact anyone. Lyle would be best, but anyone will do. Anybody that answers, get them back here on the double." He turned to Amanda. "Keep a check on the front door. Shoot anything that doesn't look human. Don't hesitate. Can you do that?"

"Piece of cake. What are you going to do?"

"Right now? I'm going to take a leak. My bladder's about to burst."

"Sure you don't need any help?"

McCoy gave Amanda the evil eye. He handed her one of the shotguns, then walked down the hallway to the restroom. The heavy wooden door took some effort to push open; he was glad it hadn't been an emergency, or he may have wet himself before he got inside.

He was concentrating on getting his stream through one of the small holes in the bottom of the urinal when he sensed something. Something Fey. He looked toward the small window. It was just big enough for a Sluagh to slip through, but there was a metal grate covering it. He finished his business and turned his attention to the three stalls which sat along the opposite wall. The doors were all closed.

He bent over and looked at the spaces under the doors. He could see no feet, but something might be crouching upon one of the toilets.

One by one, he kicked the stall doors open. Each was empty. He began to worry about Amanda. He shouldn't have left her alone to guard the door. Talbot was there, too, but he would be concentrating on the radio. He needed to get back out there. He turned to the wooden door and found himself staring into a face.

"McCoy," it said.

He jumped back in spite of himself. It was a good thing he'd just emptied his bladder.

The face on the door chuckled. "Getting old and jumpy?" it asked. It spoke in a male voice with a slight Scottish accent.

"Maybe older, but not dumber, " McCoy said as he pulled his 9mm from under his shirt. It was also loaded with specially made iron rounds. "I was wondering when the rest of you would join the party, dryad."

The dryad made a *tsk* sound and gave McCoy a look of disdain. "You would shoot the messenger bearing a white flag?"

McCoy laughed. "White flag? The Fey? You must think I've gone completely senile."

"Not at all. I've been sent to offer you assistance."

"And why would you want to do that? Your little munchkin fairies are attacking the town as we speak. I'd think the rest of you would want to sit back and enjoy the show, if not get actively involved."

Another *tsk*. "I'm sure you've thought this through, McCoy. The Sluagh have gone rogue under that human bitch's leadership. The Fey hierarchy has sanctioned none of this. What do we have to gain by our presence being exposed?"

"Okay," McCoy said, "I've thought about that. But if you're so concerned, why don't you stop them yourselves? Why did you even let it go this far?"

"Because once blood was spilled, it was out of our hands. We cannot become actively involved."

McCoy rolled his eyes and grunted. "Good God. You're as bad as the demons, with all your stupid rules." He narrowed his eyes at the dryad. "Since you can't become 'actively involved', what's to stop me from putting an iron slug through your ugly face?"

"We *can* offer some indirect aid," the dryad said quickly, perhaps sensing that McCoy was plenty serious. "Your situation is dire, McCoy. In a few hours, this town will be overrun and everyone in it dead or dying, including you. I won't lie to you and say that your demise wouldn't please us, under other circumstances. But we have much to lose, more so than someone like you could comprehend. Therefore, it is in our greater interest that you prevail."

McCoy tried to count the number of times he'd just been insulted, but gave up. "Okay, let's say you've got an ace you can slip me under the table, and I manage to deflect the brunt of this. It's still too big to cover up. People are going to see, and people are going to talk. One or two might get discounted as whackos, but half the town? I don't see any way to keep this under wraps."

"Do you know what happens to a Sluagh when it is killed?"

McCoy shrugged. "The soul is released, to hell or wherever, and the body reverts back to the image of the original person. How's that going to help? If we make it through this, we'll be up to our armpits with bodies of folks who have disappeared throughout the years."

"Maybe they didn't just disappear," the dryad said slyly. "Perhaps they joined some cult, and they've been hiding in the woods all this time. Then, for some arcane reason known only to them , they attacked the town with murderous intent."

"Oh my God," McCoy said. "That's the best you've got? No one will buy it."

"But they will believe that fairies exist?" the dryad countered. "There will be no proof to contradict your story, other than accounts from a few traumatized citizens. If anyone comes looking, they will not find us. And you will have the town officials backing you up."

McCoy felt dirty for even having this conversation. He had not actually spoken to a member of the Fey since he'd been a child, before he had realized their true nature. Now they were wanting him to jump into bed with them, after years of trying to kill him at every turn. To top it all off, the whole thing might be a ruse to make sure he did get his ticket punched.

On the other hand, what choice did he have? He didn't know how many Sluagh there actually were, but the dryad seemed to think that there were more than enough to get the job done. He couldn't hope to win out if they numbered into the hundreds. He would end up getting himself killed. He could handle that, but he couldn't handle losing Amanda. He had brought her into this, fool that he was, and he was damned well going to get her out of it. But that didn't mean there wasn't any room for negotiation.

"A truce," he said to the dryad.

"What?"

"That's the price for my help. A truce between the Fey and this town. And between the Fey and me."

"You're hardly in a position to bargain," the dryad snorted.

"Maybe. But maybe I comprehend more than you realize. If I don't stop this, and if it doesn't get covered up, the Fey's time is up in this part of the world. As much as it would please *me* to see that happen, I can't put the lives of all these people on the line. And if I can save them, what happens tomorrow? Business as usual? You start picking them off one by one again? I can't live with that. I won't."

"I'm not authorized..." the dryad began.

"Then you'd better get authorized in a hurry," McCoy said. "Otherwise, I'm going to go outside and start blasting away, and if by some chance I live through it, I'll tell everyone you're here. And I'll have people backing me up. You want my help, those are the terms."

He knew he was taking a risk, but if it worked, the payoff would be big. He just hoped the Fey were not good poker players.

"Very well," the dryad said. It did not look happy. "If you come through on your end, no further harm shall come to the people of this town. Nor to you. Our business will be...forgotten."

"Good decision," McCoy said. "Now, about this 'indirect' help..."

"Find this man and bring him here at once. The Queen will halt the attack if she knows he's here. She remembers him. She watches him walk the woods. You must make sure she knows."

"What man?" McCoy asked, but the face was gone. In its place, a single word appeared in the wood. A name. It lingered but for a moment, and then it, too, was gone.

It was long enough for McCoy to read it. Moments later, he connected the pieces of the puzzle.

The fortune cookie had been right. *Soon everything will make perfect sense.*

McCoy busted through the door and ran for the lobby.

Chapter Nine

"Baracheck!" McCoy shouted as he came out of the hallway and into the lobby.

"What?" Amanda and Talbot asked simultaneously. McCoy saw that there were now two other deputies in the room: Deidre Pratt, and a small guy that McCoy didn't know. The little guy was bleeding from a gash in his abdomen. The wound looked bad.

"Baracheck," McCoy repeated, turning to Talbot. "Sixteen, seventeen years ago, his girl went missing up on Miller's Ridge."

Talbot thought for a moment, then nodded. "Yeah. I remember that. I was a teenager. I helped with the search."

"I was out of town a lot that year, so I pretty much missed out on it," McCoy said. "But I remember it being in the papers. Damn! I should have seen this."

"The Baracheck girl is the one you saw on Drover Mountain," Amanda guessed.

"I think so. And the girl the demon showed me."

"Demon?" asked Talbot. "What demon?"

"Never mind. Would you have the girl's photo on file?"

"It might be in the database," Deidre said. "I can't get online because of the lines being down, but if it's in our local network, I can pull it up."

"Do it," McCoy said.

Deidre went to her desk and started typing on the computer keyboard. McCoy walked over to the wounded deputy.

"Looks like you've had a rough lick, Deputy..."

"Kenner," the wounded man said. "I'll be all right." He didn't look like he was going to be all right. His skin was pale, and he was leaning against a wall for support. He looked as if he ought to be dead already.

"Is there a first aid kit here?" McCoy asked.

"Yeah," Talbot replied. "I'll get one." He ducked into a closet and reappeared moments later with a small plastic box. "It isn't much," he said by way of an apology. He handed the kit to McCoy.

"McCoy turned to Amanda. "Think you can patch him up?" he asked.

"It won't be pretty, but I'll see what I can do. Cover the door?"

McCoy nodded. He saw that they had locked the doors to the main entrance, but seeing as how they were made of glass, they wouldn't withstand much of an attack.

"These two the only ones you could get a hold of?" he asked Talbot.

"Actually, Deidre was the only one who answered. Kenner came in on his own."

"No word from Lyle?"

Talbot shook his head. Despite his misgivings concerning Lyle's handling of recent events, it was apparent he was worried about the sheriff.

"Don't sweat it too much. Lyle knows what's going on, and if ever there was a man good at watching his own ass, it's him. I'm sure he's okay."

Talbot nodded, but seemed unconvinced.

"I've got it," Deidre announced. "It's an old case, so it took a little digging."

"Does it have a picture of the girl?" McCoy asked.

"Yeah. It's a little grainy, but you can make it out okay."

McCoy shot a glance at the front doors, saw nothing amiss, and went to look at the computer screen. Staring at him from the monitor's soft glow was the girl whose form the demon had taken. Add seventeen years, and he was sure it was the girl from the mountain.

"Please tell me you have a current address for the parents."

Deidre tapped on the keyboard. "The father, David, is still listed at the same address, 14238 Miller's Ridge Road. I think the mother was institutionalized, or something."

"Okay. The phones are out, so I've got to go get him."

"What? Why?" Talbot asked.

"I can't explain everything. There's no time. It'll take me a good twenty minutes to get to Miller's Ridge. Another twenty back. Assuming I only have to spend five minutes convincing Baracheck to come with me, that's forty-five minutes. We've probably got less than an hour and a half before the town's overrun."

"I'm coming with you," Amanda said.

McCoy looked at Talbot. "Can you three hold the fort down until we get back?"

Talbot shrugged. "What choice do we have? But do me a favor and keep an eye out for Lyle. I'd feel a lot better if he were here. And in charge."

McCoy slapped the deputy on the shoulder. "You're doing fine, big guy. But I'll keep my eyes peeled for the sheriff."

He set about gathering his things. He left one of the iron-loaded shotguns with Talbot, while Amanda carried the other. They stood at the front entrance and examined the night outside. All had been quiet since the last round of gunfire. McCoy didn't know if that was good or bad.

"Okay, let's do this," he said. "John, lock the doors behind us. Don't go out unless you absolutely have to. Those things are sly, and they'll try to lure you out."

"It just feels wrong," the deputy said. "Us sitting in here while people out there may need our help."

"I know it does. But Kenner needs to lie still, and someone needs to watch him. Besides, Lyle could call in or return at any time. Be patient. We'll be back as soon as we can."

McCoy unlocked the doors, and he and Amanda cautiously hurried to the truck. Before entering the vehicle, they checked the bed and peered through the windows of the cab to make sure nothing was lying in wait.

"Looks clear," McCoy said. "Hop in."

They opened the doors and climbed into the cab. McCoy fired Boo up and took off, figuring the noisy, idling truck might draw attention. He made an illegal u-turn in the middle of the street and they headed west toward Miller's Ridge Road.

The town still showed no signs of being under siege, though McCoy's senses were going into overdrive. The Sluagh were here, all right, but they were taking pains not to let their presence be known. Possibly, the bulk of the horde had not yet arrived. McCoy hoped this was the case. If he could get back with Baracheck before the main onslaught began, he might stand a chance of diffusing the situation entirely.

They sped through the night, McCoy going as fast as he dared while keeping a lookout for roadblocks or other traps. He wondered what had happened to Lyle. The man was self-serving and egocentric, but he was hardly a coward. McCoy found it hard to believe that the sheriff had either skipped town or was holed up somewhere. The bitter truth was that Lyle might be dead, and if that were the case, McCoy would have to rely on Talbot to help him sell the cover-up story to outside authorities. Assuming, of course, that they lived long enough to tell anything.

"So, how did you figure it out?" Amanda asked when they'd left the lights of the town behind them.

"It suddenly came to me," McCoy answered.

"Oh, is that so?"

"Yeah. It came to me right after a dryad appeared in the bathroom and spelled it out for me."

"What? There was a Fey in there with you? Christ, Finn! We left those three alone in there, and you didn't think to mention that the station was fairy-infested?"

"Relax. It's gone now, and it won't be back."

"And you know this how?"

"It said it wouldn't. Well, not in so many words, but..."

"And you believed it? After all the stories you've told me?"

A large dog bolted out in front of the truck, and McCoy had to swerve to narrowly miss hitting the animal. Whether the dog was chasing something or being chased, he couldn't tell.

"I've brokered a truce," McCoy said. "As long as we can stop the Sluagh and keep the outside world from finding out about the Fey, they've agreed to leave the town alone. And me."

"Have you totally lost it? Do you think for one minute that they'll honor those terms?" Amanda asked, unbelieving.

"Maybe not. Hell, probably not. But there's a chance they might, at least for a while. The Fey are evil and cruel, but they live by a different code than we do." He turned to her and grinned. "Anyway, it was worth a shot, and I do love tormenting them."

"Well, if we can't get this Baracheck to return to town with us, it'll all be a moot point."

"Listen, I know this is going to sound cruel, but we can't let Baracheck in on the whole story. For one thing, we just don't have the time. For another, it will be too much for him to comprehend on such short notice."

"So what do we do?" Amanda asked. "Knock him over the head and drag him back?"

"Nothing that drastic. I hope. We simply tell him that we've found his daughter."

"And get his hopes up, only to see them dashed when he discovers she's now the leader of a pack of maniacal fairies? How can we do that? That poor man has been suffering for seventeen years."

"I told you it was going to sound bad," McCoy said. "And I guess maybe it *is* bad, but what else can we do? We have to look at the big picture. If we don't get Baracheck back into Shallow Springs before all hell breaks loose, a lot of people are going to die."

"I'd still rather knock him over the head," Amanda sulked.

"I guess it's an option," McCoy conceded, and went back to concentrating on the road.

***

Lyle was growing impatient. It had never taken the dryad this long to show up before. He was certain that he'd used the right words. They were the same words he had uttered before, on several occasions, and always the fairy had appeared within minutes.

Dealing with the Fey was something he had no taste for, and he would have been drawn and quartered before admitting that he had ever done so. No one knew, not even McCoy. Especially McCoy. That man already held a low opinion of him, and if McCoy ever found out that Lyle had conspired with the Fey—not once, but on several occasions—he would have done everything in his power to see to it that Lyle was removed from office, at the very least.

He didn't understand why this was happening. He had always worked with the Fey to ensure that conditions were favorable to both parties involved. They helped keep him in office by dissuading or removing his opposition, and he turned a blind eye when someone went missing every so often. As long as it wasn't a friend of his—and it never was; he'd seen to that—he counted it as an acceptable loss.

And then the little ugly ones had gone rogue. Lyle, of course, had summoned the dryad after the first two murders, only to be told that there was nothing they could do. Their hands were tied, some sort of damn fairy protocol. *Bring in McCoy*, the dryad had said, and like an idiot, Lyle had done so. Now, his town was about to be turned into an all-you-can-eat buffet, and McCoy wasn't doing jack shit about it.

On the tree closest to the sheriff, the bark began to ripple. The dryad's face appeared, its wooden eyes regarding Lyle with condescension. Lyle would have given almost anything to slap the bark off of its ugly face.

"It's about time," the sheriff said harshly. "The lambs are about to go to the slaughter, and McCoy is useless. Something has to be done."

"Something *is* being done, Good Sheriff," the dryad said in a bored tone." As we speak, McCoy is on his way to fetch the girl's father."

"Dave Baracheck? What good is he going to do?"

"She won't launch an attack if he's in harm's way. We've been watching her, and she's been watching him. She *remembers*."

"That's it?" Lyle was beside himself. "That's all it's gonna take? Hell, *I* could have done that. Why bring McCoy in on this at all?"

Even as he said it, Lyle began to have a bad feeling. He was certain that he'd missed something, and it had led to him making a grave error in judgment. The dryad looked at him, its wooden eyebrows arched, awaiting more.

"There's something more," Lyle said slowly. "Something you aren't telling me."

"You know what we see fit for you to know," the dryad said haughtily. "Don't make the mistake of putting us on equal ground."

Lyle wanted to tell the tree spirit to stick it where the sun doesn't shine, but he sensed he was already treading on unsteady ground. If it hadn't been critical that McCoy be involved, then that meant the fairies had *wanted* him involved. The question was why? Lyle disliked McCoy; the Fey hated him with a vengeance. McCoy had killed a Fey of some importance when he'd been nineteen or twenty, and the fairies had been out to get him ever since.

"It's a trap," the sheriff reasoned. "You could have stopped this all along. You wanted me to bring McCoy back here so you could get at him."

"No. We have not lied to you about the Sluagh. They must be stopped by forces outside the Fey. That is just the way things are."

"Bullshit. McCoy..."

"McCoy is going to come to no harm," the dryad interjected, its voice threatening. "Not

by the hands of the Fey, not just yet. Do you know the lifespan of our species, Sheriff?"

Lyle said nothing, because he had no idea.

"When I was young, your ancestors were using rocks and sticks and living in huts. We can afford to let McCoy live a little while longer, especially since we've recently found a use for him."

"What kind of use?" Lyle asked. He didn't like the way the dryad was looking at him.

"If McCoy is successful, he will be looked upon as a hero by the people of the town. He will hold influence. They will listen to his opinions."

Lyle was confused. "I'd think that would be the last thing you'd want. What if he decides to spill the beans about the Fey?"

"He won't. We have already made an agreement with Mr. McCoy."

"You what? Behind my back?"

One of the trees limbs shot out and twisted itself around Lyle's neck. Gasping for air, he grabbed his sidearm and emptied it into the tree. Since the bullets were traditional lead rounds, they had no effect.

"You have outlived your effectiveness," the dryad spat at him. "Before the next sun sets, there will be a new sheriff, handpicked by Finn McCoy, and born of the Fey."

Lyle had just enough time to wonder who that might be, and then the branch constricted violently, snapping his neck.

Chapter Ten

"Pull closer to the mailbox," Amanda said. "I can't quite make out the name."

McCoy eased the truck closer to the rusty mailbox. It would have been difficult to read the faded paint in the middle of the day, but they could make out the last four letters: *heck.*

"This has to be it," McCoy said. He angled into the gravel driveway and headed for the house. No lights shown through any of the windows. He pulled up to the house and left the lights and motor running.

"Should I take the shotgun?" Amanda asked.

"No, better leave it in the truck. Around here, someone comes banging on your door at four AM holding a gun, you shoot first and ask questions later. If worse comes to worst, I've got the nine in my pants."

"Remind me to make a joke about that later." Amanda opened the door and hopped out.

McCoy climbed from the driver's seat and they walked toward the house. It was a cozy ranch-style, with cedar siding to give it a rustic, cabin-like appearance. The front lawn was spacious, though somewhat neglected.

"What are those?" Amanda asked as they reached the front door. Hanging from nails which had been hammered in above the door frame were several small figures. They appeared to be made of grass or straw.

"Poppets," McCoy said. "Folk magic dolls, used for protection. Obviously, Baracheck has some idea of what happened to his daughter."

"They're hanging over all of the windows, too. There must be forty or fifty of those little buggers."

McCoy fondled one of the poppets. He was beginning to get an idea. But first things first. They needed to rouse Baracheck. McCoy searched for a doorbell, found none, and instead rapped sharply on the front door.

No sound came from inside the house, and no lights flickered on. McCoy knocked again, harder.

"Whoever you are, you'd better have a damned good reason for banging on my door at this time of night."

The voice hadn't come from within the house. It had come from directly behind them. Amanda jumped and gave an involuntary squeal.

McCoy turned slowly and saw just what he'd expected to see: a shotgun barrel stuck in his face. Baracheck was a few feet behind them, standing in the yard.

"If you're David Baracheck, then yes, we have a good reason. It's about your daughter, Cynthia."

Baracheck stiffened, and he let the gun drop slightly, but he didn't go as far as pointing it away from McCoy. "Cynthie?' he asked.

"Yes sir," McCoy said. "If you'd be so kind as to point that scattergun someplace else, we need to talk."

Baracheck's expression was conflicted. He didn't know these people, but they apparently knew about him and his missing daughter. Suspicion and curiosity waged a war within him. In the end, of course, the need to know won out. He lowered the gun.

"Is she dead?" Baracheck cut straight to the chase. McCoy realized that the man had spent years preparing himself for this very moment. Looking at the man's face, he wished he had happier news. While Cynthia was very much alive, she was , in all likelihood, dead to her father. She had, after all, been abducted at a very young age. McCoy didn't see how she would have anything but a few vague memories of her life before the Sluagh. The head-knocking option was looking better all the time.

"No, she's alive. That's why we're here in the middle of the night. We need you to come back with us, to the Springs."

Whatever reaction McCoy had been expecting, Dave Baracheck didn't give. He simply nodded slowly, as if trying to understand McCoy's words. Then he began to sway on his feet, and McCoy realized that the man was on the verge of fainting. He caught Baracheck by the arm just as the man began to sink to his knees.

"Help me," McCoy grunted to Amanda. "Let's get him on the porch."

Amanda rushed over and took Baracheck by the other arm. Together, they managed to walk the stricken man up the small flight of steps and onto the porch. They lowered him into a padded rocker, where he sat, looking confused and unbelieving.

"Mr. Baracheck," McCoy said, "I know this is unexpected, and probably overwhelming, but we really need to get back to town as quickly as possible."

"All these years," Baracheck mumbled. "I didn't think I'd given up hope, but I guess I had." His eyes cleared somewhat, and he looked at McCoy. "Someone took her, didn't they? All this time I've been thinking that it was those things in the woods. But she must have been with *someone*, right? I mean, how else could she have survived?"

"Mr. Baracheck…"

"Did they get the son of a bitch? Please tell me they got him. And Cynthie, is she all right?"

"The sooner we get back to Shallow Springs," Amanda said in a calm, soothing voice, "the sooner your questions will be answered, Mr. Baracheck."

Baracheck looked at Amanda, seeming to notice her for the first time. "Dave," he said. "Call me Dave."

McCoy gave Amanda a look of gratitude. She had been able to get though to Baracheck.

"Do you need to get anything before we go?" Amanda asked.

"No. I just want to see my girl. I guess I'd better grab my keys and lock up, though."

"Mr. Baracheck, would you happen to have a few large trash bags?" McCoy asked.

Baracheck gave McCoy a puzzled look. "I guess so. Why do you want them?"

"It won't take long, I promise," McCoy said. "But we do actually have to pack a few things before we go."

Amanda looked questioningly at McCoy. All she got in return was a wink and a smile.

***

The woman once known as Cynthie to her doting father stood on a hill and looked over the still-sleeping town. Very soon the rest of the horde would join her. The sun would start to rise in about three hours; there was plenty of time to do what needed to be done.

Already, some of the others were in the town, clearing the way for the main group's advance. By the time they arrived, the police force would be either diminished or decimated. They would encounter little resistance.

There were only two rules concerning the incursion, and she was fairly certain that they would be followed. The first was that no children would be harmed or taken. This had been law since she had first taken leadership, and it had never been violated.

The second was that the sheriff was not to be touched. This order was puzzling to the others, but since there would be so many others to prey upon, they had not questioned it. If they had, she would not have bothered to explain herself, anyway. She had her reasons, and that was all they needed to know.

The truth was that the sheriff was not to be harmed because the sheriff was hers. She alone would snuff out the life of the man who had allowed her to be taken, and in turn had taken everything from her.

As for the rest of the adults, who among them was blameless? They had looked for her, but not hard enough. They had not rescued her. They had left her to fend for herself, and in that, at least, she had not failed herself. She had survived, and then thrived, and had finally dominated. But by then it had been too late. She'd thought of slipping away from the others; it would have been easy by then. She'd found, however, that she had neither the ability nor the desire to reintegrate into society. They had done nothing for her, and they had done nothing for her poor father. Both of them had been left to wither and die by the people of the town.

But she had learned. At her direction, the others had captured an adult. They had kept the woman alive for nearly a year, and during that time Cynthia had learned the language and ways of the townspeople.

She turned and saw the rest of the horde approaching. Down the mountain they came, ugly and malformed little creatures with nothing in their souls but hate and an insatiable appetite for blood. Watching them advance, she realized that she was just like them; maybe not outwardly, but on the inside, at least. She had become a monster. The thought occurred to her that it didn't have to be that way, but she brushed it aside with a cold indifference. The die had been cast. Her fate was as immalleable now as it had been seventeen years ago, when she had been taken from her warm bed in the middle of the night.

She turned her attention back to the town. Let the fools suffer. Let them know the horror she had known all those years ago. It would be justice, pure and simple.

Justice would be coming to Shallow Springs within the hour.

***

Big John Talbot checked his watch. Though the town had remained quiet after the first initial bursts of gunfire, John had the feeling that time was running out, that an avalanche was barreling down the mountain, and that soon the town would be buried underneath it.

He wished McCoy would return. He wished Lyle would show up. Hell, he wished *anyone* would show up and take matters out of his hands.

John had always been a good officer, but he was not accustomed to being in the position of leadership. He was good at following orders, but when it came to giving them, he was uncertain and prone to second-guessing himself. Lyle had made it look easy.

If he were serious about his aspiration to one day become sheriff, however, he knew this was a test that he must pass. Deep down, he was certain that he had the ability to take control, but he had assumed that he would have years to hone the talent before he would actually have to use it. Now that circumstances had thrust the situation upon him, though, it was do or die.

On the upside, Kenner's condition seemed to be actually improving. John didn't know how that was possible, because the man's wound looked awful and he had obviously lost a lot of blood. Nonetheless, Kenner was up and moving around with little or no assistance at all. This was good, because if there was a battle coming, John would need all of the manpower he could get a hold of. To this end, he had considered trying to round up some of the citizens who lived nearby. But McCoy had told him to stay put, and so far, he had.

McCoy seemed to have some type of plan. John sure hoped it was a good one. He really didn't want to tangle with one of the creatures he'd seen back on Duncan Road, much less a whole slew of them. He couldn't wrap his head around the fact that those things actually existed. John had lived in Shallow Springs all his life. He had roamed the back roads as a teenager and had hunted the mountains since he'd been old enough to carry a rifle. Never in his wildest imagination had he thought that the woods might harbor real monsters.

The fact that Lyle had obviously known about them was even more disquieting, and it begged another question: *how long* had he known? John would have been deliriously happy to think that the sheriff had only recently discovered their existence, but he didn't honestly believe that to be the case. And if Lyle had known all along that those things were out there, why hadn't he done anything about it? Where was the National Guard? Where were the freaking Marines? Lyle hadn't even confided in his own deputies, for Christ's sake.

All of this left a foul odor which smelled a lot like a conspiracy. Shallow Springs had more unsolved disappearances per capita than any other town or city in the state, with the possible exception of Richmond. If these creatures were involved in at least some of the vanishings, and if Lyle had known about it and had chosen to remain silent, then he was, at the very least, an accessory.

John could think of only two reasons why Lyle would keep such information to himself: either the sheriff was scared, or he was getting something in return. And John didn't think Lyle was scared of much of anything at all.

If and when Lyle returned, John knew that he would have to confront the sheriff with his suspicions. He could not, in good conscience, continue to work for a man who had been even passively involved with the deaths of citizens he was sworn to protect. Though he hated the thought of leaving his chosen profession, he would if it came down to it. But it might not. There was a chance that John might be able to coerce Lyle into retirement, leaving the door open for John himself to seek the position.

To do this, though, he would need either proof or an admission of guilt, and both were currently in short supply. Not to mention, all of this was assuming that they lived to see dawn, and that, by John's best guess, was a big "if".

"It's nagging at you, isn't it?" Kenner said from behind him. John nearly jumped through the roof.

"Sorry," the smaller man said. "Didn't mean to startle you."

"It's okay. I guess we're all on edge. How're you feeling, Paul.?"

"Better, now that I've had a chance to rest."

John looked doubtfully at Kenner's wound. The makeshift bandage job was already red with blood. "We need to get you to the hospital as soon as we can," he said.

Kenner dismissed the suggestion with a wave of his hand. It was a gesture John had never seen the man make before.

"We've got bigger fish to fry here, Big John. Like what to do about Lyle, for instance."

"What about Lyle?"

Kenner looked around to see where Deidre was. The female deputy was over at the dispatch station, toying with the radio. Seemingly satisfied, Kenner leaned toward John and spoke in a low voice.

"The fact that Lyle is in cahoots with those gremlins. It's obvious to me, and I think you know it , too."

John grabbed his jaw and pretended to rub it to keep it from hitting the floor. Kenner had never been the sharpest knife in the drawer. The only reason he'd gotten this job was that his uncle was a councilman, and everyone, including Paul Kenner, knew it. He was a likeable little guy, but he wasn't much of an officer. John knew for a fact that Lyle despised Kenner. How Kenner had suddenly mustered the insight to reach his conclusion was beyond John's ability to reckon.

"It's obvious to you?" John asked, not sure how he should play this.

"Of course," Kenner replied with another dismissive wave. "He had to know that those things were out there, and he had to have some kind of deal going with them. Otherwise, they would have raided the town before now."

"What makes you think that?"

Kenner looked at John as if the big man had just crawled drooling from under a cabbage leaf. "Look at the number of disappearances we've had over the years. You mean to stand there and tell me that those things weren't responsible for some of them, if not all? Lyle's not stupid. He's known for years, I'll bet."

John wasn't sure he liked being talked down to by someone a foot and a half shorter than he was, but he kept his cool. Kenner was injured and probably not in a right frame of mind. Maybe that was why he was acting funny. On the flipside, the injury sure had made the little guy a lot smarter.

"I'll bet you're wondering what Lyle got out of turning the other way," Kenner said.

"The question had crossed my mind," John admitted.

"How long has Lyle been Sheriff?" Kenner asked. "Twenty-some odd years? And that with two or three people going missing every year. None of them ever solved. Not much of a track record to use as a platform for re-election, is it?"

John had to admit that Kenner was right. He had never really thought much about it before, but it did seem odd that Lyle had been able to hold onto his job without ever solving a missing persons case. And because major crimes were not prevalent in Shallow Springs, each case had been a pretty big deal. But Lyle had always had some explanation. This one ran off with a girl two towns over. Another owed a bunch of drug money and left town. More than a few were probably victims of wild animal attacks. And so on. Since there had never before been any real evidence of foul play, people tended to accept whatever explanation the sheriff offered.

"Remember a few years back when Tom Baker was running against Lyle?" Kenner asked. "Early polls showed Baker had the job in the bag. Then he suddenly withdrew and he and his family left town in a hurry. Everyone suspected that Lyle had something on Baker. Maybe he did, only it wasn't what everybody thought. You know what I mean?"

John knew exactly. It all made perfect sense. He still didn't know how Kenner had figured more of this out than he himself had, but he had to admit that the little guy was certainly on the ball.

"So," Kenner said. "What are you going to do?"

"Me?"

"Yeah, you. You're the senior deputy. Not only that, but everyone respects you. If anyone's going to set this right, it has to be you."

"I guess that depends," John said.

"On what?"

"On whether or not Lyle returns. He's been out of contact for a long time. That's not like him. He likes to be in control."

Kenner grinned. It looked out of place on his pale, sweaty face. "Yeah," he said, "you're right. You are the sharp one, Big John. Maybe they've already taken Lyle out. Poetic justice, wouldn't you say?"

"I'd say no one deserves to die like that. Not at the hands of those...whatever they are."

"Did all those people who vanished over the years deserve it?"

"No, of course not."

"Then if Lyle was a part of it, it's justice." Kenner turned and checked on Deidre, who was still back at dispatch. "You need to start thinking about yourself, and what's next for you," he said, turning back to John. "If Lyle's out of the picture, the council will put you in as interim sheriff. It's a done deal."

John hadn't really thought that far ahead, but he supposed it was true. Lyle still had over a year left before the next election. The town council would almost certainly appoint him to fill in until then, but he would have to bust his ass to win the general election in November. With Lyle gone, he would be certain to face some stiff opposition. Opposition with big money backing them.

As if reading his mind, Kenner said, "The next election will be tough. A lot of people around here have been waiting patiently for Lyle to slip up or retire. You'll need the right kind of backing to ensure the job will be yours."

"I assume you know where I might find that backing?" John asked.

Kenner's grin became a full-fledged smile, and John didn't much care for it. "I do believe that I can be of assistance, John."

"You're talking about your uncle?"

For a moment Kenner's expression went blank, as if he had no idea what John was talking about. Then the smile was back, but he was shaking his head.

"Oh, John," Kenner laughed. "That's small fish. I'm talking about a major player here. With someone like this behind you, you couldn't lose even if you tried. Of course, there will have to be a minor concession on your part, but..."

"Someone's here!" Deidre shouted. John turned to the front doors. Sure enough, he could see a pair of headlights pull up in front of the building. He turned back to Kenner.

"We'll talk later, Paul." Kenner looked annoyed, but nodded in agreement.

"C'mon," John said. "It appears we have company."

Chapter Eleven

"Is she here?" Baracheck asked as McCoy pulled to a stop in front of the sheriff's office.

"Let's get inside, then we'll talk," McCoy said. He had an urgent feeling, like time was growing short, and he didn't like being out in the open. "Amanda, cover us on the way in. I'm going to get those bags out of the bed."

Amanda nodded and got out of the truck. Baracheck, who had been sitting between them, followed her out. McCoy swung out of the driver's side and hauled the two large trash bags out of the bed of the truck. The contents of the bags rustled as he hurried up the sidewalk to the front doors of the building.

John Talbot was fumbling with the door locks as they approached. He got the doors open just as they made it to the entrance, and the three of them hurried inside. Talbot locked the doors behind them.

"Where's Cynthie?" Baracheck asked when they were all safely inside. "I want to see my daughter. I want to see my daughter now."

Talbot started to say something, but McCoy shot him a warning glance. He took Baracheck by the arm and gently steered the man toward Lyle's office.

"Where are we going?" Baracheck asked.

"To talk."

Baracheck stopped in his tracks. "Mr. McCoy, I've been more than patient so far. But that patience is wearing thin. I think I have a right to know what's going on here."

"You're right," McCoy said. "Let's go into the office. I'll tell you everything I know, and then you can decide whether or not you want to be a part of this. I've got to warn you, though; it may be a little late to walk away."

"If it involves Cynthie, Mr. McCoy, there's no way in hell I'm walking away."

McCoy nodded, and they went into the office. McCoy shut the door behind them.

"Have a seat, Mr. Baracheck," McCoy said. Baracheck took one of the chairs that sat in front of the large desk. McCoy took the other one.

"My daughter's not here, is she?"

"In this building? No. But I haven't lied to you, Mr. Baracheck. She is alive. I saw her myself, only yesterday."

"Call me Dave. Where were you when you saw her?"

"I was driving up Drover Mountain."

"And how do you know it was Cynthia, Mr. McCoy? I haven't seen my daughter in seventeen years. I might pass her on the street and not recognize her."

McCoy paused as he considered how to continue. "Back at your house, when I told you that Cynthia was alive, you said something about thinking that the things in the woods took her. What do you know about those things, Dave?"

Baracheck shrugged. "I don't know what they are. I've never really gotten a good look at one, but I've caught glimpses, and I've heard them. I know that the grass monkeys seem to keep them away."

"Grass monkeys? You mean the poppets?"

"Whatever. I got them from an old man named Dalton. He died several years back. His wife made them, I think."

"Okay," McCoy said. "I'm going to give you a really brief rundown on the situation. It has to be quick, because we haven't got much time. The things that kidnapped your daughter are called the Sluagh. You can think of them as evil spirits or monsters; it doesn't really matter. The Sluagh enjoy two things: killing adults and abducting children. They're proficient at both. Whatever happens to the children, most of them are never seen again. For some reason, this isn't the case with Cynthia."

Baracheck shook his head. "I don't understand. What you seem to be telling me is that not only is my daughter alive, but that she has been here in Shallow Springs all this time. If those things took her, how could she have survived? Why hasn't she come home, or at least contacted me?"

"I asked myself those same questions," McCoy said, "and I believe I have the answer. You're not going to particularly like it, though."

"I didn't figure I would."

"Cynthia is alive because the Sluagh took care of her. I don't know why they did. It goes against everything I know about the creatures. Whatever the reason, they are her family now, and I have every reason to believe that she is leading the pack."

Baracheck took a moment to digest this information. Outwardly he appeared to remain calm, but McCoy knew that the man was struggling with conflicting emotions. On one hand, his daughter was alive, against all odds. At the same time, the life that she had been forced to live might have made death seem like a more humane option.

"I assume," Baracheck said slowly, as if each word held a great weight, "that there's a reason that you drug me into town at this hour. I mean, as important as this news is to me, I'm sure you would have waited until morning unless you had a good reason not to."

"You're right, of course. That brings us to the next part. I said that Cynthia isn't in this building, and that's true. But she *is* in town, or if not, she will be soon."

"If she's with those things, why would she be coming here?"

"Because she's leading the Sluagh on an attack on the town."

Baracheck gave McCoy a look of pure contempt. "You're out of your mind. Cynthie would never do something like that. I don't care what's happened to her over the years, my daughter would not spill the blood of innocent people."

"Dave, you're thinking of her as a three year-old girl. She's not, and hasn't been for a long time."

"It doesn't matter!" Baracheck yelled. "She doesn't have it in her. When she was little, she wouldn't even step on an ant. All I've heard here so far is conjecture and supposition. And while part of me hopes that Cynthia is alive, another part hopes to God that you're nothing more than a raving lunatic, Mr. McCoy."

McCoy looked down at his hands. "I wish I were, too, Mr. Baracheck. It would make things easier for a lot of people. But since I'm fairly certain I'm as sane as the next guy, I need to tell you why I brought you into town."

Baracheck said nothing. He was staring at one of the trophy fish on Lyle's wall.

"She remembers you," McCoy said.

Baracheck looked at him then, and McCoy saw that tears welled in the man's eyes. It certainly didn't make going on any easier, but he had no choice.

"I'm not the only one who's seen Cynthia. She's been spotted watching you as you walked through the forest. I don't know how much she remembers, but she knows who you are. And that's why you have to be here, in town. She won't attack if she knows you're here. She won't risk you getting hurt."

Baracheck broke down then. His eyes were closed tightly and his body was racked by the force of his silent sobs. McCoy tried to imagine how the man must feel, but found that he couldn't. He didn't have children, and he had never, before Amanda, let himself get close to anyone. Still, it was a hard thing to watch, and he was relieved when Baracheck began to pull himself together.

"I'm sorry," Baracheck said when he was able to speak.

"Don't be."

"So what are the chances of this having a happy ending?"

"I can't say."

"Can't, or won't?"

McCoy looked the man in the eyes. "I've seen a lot of things in my time, Dave. A little too much to say that this can't work out good, and way too much to sit here and tell you that it will. A lot of it depends on Cynthia. We can't know what living with the Sluagh for years has done to her mind. But maybe, just maybe, the memories of her time with you will be enough to bring her back."

"I pray to God that they will," Baracheck said. "I've missed her so."

"I'm sure you have. And you have my word that she will not be harmed if at all possible."

Baracheck nodded. "I appreciate that. But let's be clear on one thing before we do this. I'll do what you want me to, but my main concern is getting my little girl back."

"I couldn't see it being any other way," McCoy said, and they got up to rejoin the rest of the group.

***

Sam Henderson stared at the coffee maker, or tried to. His eyes kept shutting; he should have known better than to sit up and watch that stupid movie last night. It had been one of those chick flicks that Carolyn liked to watch, and she had wanted him to watch it with her. It had actually been a pretty good movie, but he had pretended not to like it out of principle.

Sam was not a morning person by nature, but the Triple Gem Mining Company was doing its damndest to make him one. The job was a double jinx; he had to get up early, and he had to work underground. Neither situation greatly appealed to him, but coal mining was pretty much the only good-paying job that you could get with just a high school diploma, unless you moved away. Sam had been born and raised in Shallow Springs and had no intention of leaving, thus he was resigned but since he already had the shotgun and flashlight, he might as well take a quick look-see. At least he would feel better about leaving Carolyn there alone.

Sam opened the door and peered out into the blackness. Nothing moved, which was odd because Rusty usually came running when he heard a door open. Surely the dog hadn't gone off in pursuit of whatever it was that had spooked him. Rusty was territorial; he guarded the yard as if he owned it, but he wasn't prone to wandering off. He called for the dog. Like Carolyn, Rusty did not respond.

Well, it wasn't getting any earlier. He had five minutes, tops, before he had to leave. Even though they lived only a few minutes from town, he had to pass through the Springs and travel another fifteen minutes to get to the mine. He hadn't been late since he'd started the day shift, and he wasn't about to tarnish his record.

He walked out onto the small back porch and again called Rusty's name. No dice. It wasn't like the mutt not to come when Sam called, either. He wasn't as much concerned as aggravated; he was sure Rusty would come dragging home with his tail between his legs sooner or later. He listened for a moment, heard nothing out of the ordinary, and started back inside.

Something hit his legs, hard and low, and he grabbed the door frame to keep from tumbling over. He looked down to see a naked kid wrapped around his legs. Except it was a funny-looking kid, the way its backbone arched, and it stank to high hell. Then it bit into his leg. The pain was tremendous, but he didn't concentrate on it for long because another one jumped on his back and sank its teeth into his shoulder. He tried to swing the shotgun around, but it was torn from his grasp and lost to him.

More of the kids-that-weren't-kids piled onto him, driving him to his knees. He saw several of them run through the door and into the house. He tried to scream for Carolyn, to tell her to lock the bedroom door and call the police, but all that came out was a strangled gurgle.

The last thing that Sam heard was a single, startled scream from his wife. Then his world fell silent.

Chapter Twelve

"It's time to go," McCoy said to the five people circling him. "If we wait any longer, a lot of people are going to die."

"Finally," Big John said. "I'm tired of being holed up like a scared rabbit." He checked his sidearm for the hundredth time and, satisfied, shoved it back in the holster.

"Remember," McCoy said, "regular ammo will slow them down, but it won't kill them. Use the shotgun I brought when you're in close and know you've got a killshot. And don't forget that we have limited ammo, so please don't waste it firing at shadows."

Big John carried one of McCoy's shotguns, while Amanda had the other. McCoy had given his 9mm to Deidre, and was himself carrying the black rowan walking stick. Kenner had declined any type of weapon since his wounds made him pretty much useless in a fight. The plan was for him to hang back and act as a spotter, so that none of the others would be ambushed from their blind sides.

Baracheck was also unarmed, but he would be in the least danger of being attacked as long as Cynthia was present. Since their plan was to find and confront her, her presence was all but guaranteed.

They had decided to travel in one vehicle, and since the cruisers would not accommodate six people, Boo was the obvious choice. Three people could sit in the cab, while the other three rode in the bed. Those three would be more vulnerable and exposed, but they would also be armed the heaviest.

"They'll come in from the north," McCoy said as they prepared to leave. "We'll ride out to where the houses start. If we don't encounter them on the road, we'll wait for them there. John, make sure we have plenty of lights. And whatever you do, don't forget the bullhorn."

"Got it covered," John replied.

"Dave, give me a hand with those trash bags," said McCoy.

They opened the front doors and began to file toward the waiting truck. McCoy pulled Amanda to the side.

"I'd rather have you up front with me," he said.

"We've been through this, Finn. Baracheck and Kenner are up front. I can handle the shotgun just fine, and I'll have two cops with me."

"I realize that. But if the Sluagh attack, it'll be like a swarm of ants."

"That's only if we get caught in the middle of them. I'm trusting you not to let that happen."

"Right. Put all the pressure on me." He gave her a serious look. "Just be careful, okay?"

"Every chance I get," she said, and gave him a quick kiss.

They sprinted to the truck. Amanda hopped into the bed with John and Deidre. McCoy and Baracheck tossed the trash bags into the bed, then scampered into the cab. McCoy pulled into the street and headed north. There was no sign of life as they sped through the town, human or otherwise.

Kenner was sandwiched between McCoy and Baracheck. The smaller man seemed nervous, and he kept glancing at McCoy.

"Something on your mind, Deputy?" McCoy asked when he could no longer stand it.

"They say you're a spook-hunter or something," Kenner replied.

"Or something, yeah."

"So, you can see ghosts?"

"Sometimes, when they want me to." McCoy took a curve as fast as he dared. He checked the rearview mirror to make sure he hadn't slung anyone out.

"And you can, like, sense their presence?"

"I guess," McCoy said somewhat irritably. "Is there a point to this? I've got a lot on my plate at the moment, in case you hadn't noticed."

"Yeah. I mean, I know. It's just that...if I don't make it through this, I'd like to think that there's something more. That this isn't the end. I figured if anyone might have an insight into that, you would."

McCoy sighed. "Listen, I don't know exactly what happens when we die. I do know that the soul lives on, and I know that there are other worlds besides this one. Maybe you can find some peace in that."

Kenner looked at McCoy for a moment, then smiled. "Yeah, I guess I can find peace in that."

"Good," McCoy said. He suddenly needed to know that he'd remembered to bring his knapsack with him. He looked down and saw it nestled in the passenger floorboard behind Baracheck's feet.

"Look out!" Baracheck yelled, and McCoy looked up to see that the road was blocked by a fallen tree. He hit the brakes hard, causing Amanda and Deidre to slam into the rear of the cab.

"Everyone okay?" McCoy yelled.

"Yeah," Amanda said. "But give us a little warning the next time you want to do a brake check."

"What do you think?" John asked.

"I think this isn't the best place to make a stand," McCoy replied. "The woods are too close. I'm gonna back down the road a bit, find us a spot with some more breathing room."

"Better rethink that," Deidre said.

McCoy looked into the side mirror and saw that the road behind them was filed with Sluagh. Of Cynthia, he saw no sign.

"Shit! Dave, we need you visible. Kenner, stay here and make sure they don't sneak in from the other direction." McCoy grabbed his walking stick and hopped out of the cab.

The Sluagh were about fifty yards behind the truck. McCoy couldn't get a reliable count in the dark, but he was sure there were fifty or sixty of them, at least. The creatures made no move to attack, but stood watching the group with obvious interest.

"Is she here?" Baracheck asked. "Does anyone see her?"

"All I see is a bunch of little uglies," John said.

"She has to be here," McCoy said. "John, hand me the bullhorn."

John tossed the bullhorn to McCoy. He raised it to his mouth, then paused. Something wasn't right. The Sluagh could see that they were armed, but they couldn't know about the iron ammo. Likewise, the trash bags were hidden safely in the bed of the truck. The creatures had them outnumbered ten to one, yet still they hesitated. There had to be a reason, but he couldn't see it.

And then, suddenly, he did. He had been outplayed. The horde had known that they were coming, and had known that Baracheck was with them. The creatures had scouts back in town, but McCoy had never dreamed that they would be able to communicate so effectively and quickly.

They were no longer between the horde and the town. The sly creatures had let them pass through, and now their path into town was unobstructed.

As if confirming McCoy's suspicion, the Sluagh turned their backs to the group and began to move down the road toward the town.

"Damnit!" McCoy hissed. "We've got to get back in front of them."

"And how do we do that?" John asked. "They're blocking the road."

"We'll roll right through them if we have to. We have to block their assault, and we can't do that from this side."

"We might be able to slip past them," John said. "A thousand feet back down the road there's open fields on both sides. Your truck has four wheel-drive."

"Good idea," McCoy agreed. "We'll give them a few minute's head start."

"Won't they be protecting their rear flank?" Amanda asked.

"I'm sure they will, but we don't have another choice. If this tree weren't blocking the road, we'd be able to loop back to town, but it's too heavy to move and I don't have enough room to get around it."

"Can't we just pick them off from the back side?" Deidre asked. "We've got enough ammo to thin their ranks quite a bit."

"What we saw was probably only a fraction of the main force," McCoy said. "I don't think Cynthia is even with this group. If there's even twice as many, we wouldn't stand a chance. We have to get Baracheck in their path, or we'll lose the town."

Behind them, Boo began to cough and shudder.

"Kenner?" McCoy called. "What's going on?"

"I don't know," Kenner shouted. "The temperature light's flashing."

McCoy ran back to the truck and climbed into the cab just as Boo gave one final cough, spat a puff of gray smoke, and died. He tried several times to restart the truck with no success.

"You've got to be kidding me!" he yelled. He looked at Kenner, who shrugged apologetically.

"Looks like we're on foot," John said.

"Yeah, and we're going to have to make tracks," McCoy agreed. The whole situation was deteriorating at a rapid pace, and the chances of coming through it without losing more people were dwindling. On foot, they would almost certainly be ambushed by the Sluagh, and while Baracheck might escape unharmed, the rest of them didn't have the luxury of being Cynthia's father.

"All right," he said to the others. "Here's the best Plan B I can come up with on short notice. We're not going to be able to get through them or around them on foot, so we need to draw them back."

"How do we do that?" Amanda asked. "Baracheck's right where Cynthia wants him: behind the lines. She wouldn't compromise her position unless he was in danger."

McCoy considered her words. He was getting an idea, but it was a hell of a long shot, and it would have to be executed flawlessly to work. The key was getting Cynthia to think that her father was in danger. He and the others could pretend to threaten him with their weapons, but there were two problems with that scenario. First, it would probably come off as fake and unbelievable. Second, if Cynthia *did* buy it, she would simply sic the horde upon them, and if that happened, everyone—with the exception of Baracheck—would have a really bad day.

Fortunately, there was a wild card at play, and one that only McCoy knew about. The others in the group would not have to fake surprise, because they *would* be surprised, and that would give the whole thing an air of authenticity. The unknown in the equation was how Cynthia would react, but McCoy was willing to bet that she would act to save her father.

"My dear," he said to Amanda, "Your beauty is rivaled only by your genius."

Amanda raised her eyebrows in question, but McCoy gave her only a wink and quick smile.

"Okay, listen up everyone. We need to act fast. John, give Dave the shotgun and help me with those trash bags. Everyone else get ready to move out. We've got to catch up with the horde."

"What about me?" Kenner asked. "Can I come?"

"You bet your sweet life you can."

McCoy ran to the passenger side of the truck and retrieved his knapsack. He made a quick check of the contents and, satisfied, slung the bag across his shoulder. He then grabbed one of the trash bags out of the truck's bed. John handed Baracheck the shotgun and hefted the remaining bag.

"What's in the bags?" he asked McCoy.

"Presents for the Sluagh. Feel like Santa?"

"Not nearly as jolly."

"You will, later. Come on, let's get a move on."

McCoy slipped the bullhorn's strap around his wrist and picked up his walking stick. He started down the road at a brisk pace and the others followed.

***

Cynthia was pleased with herself.

She had outfoxed the Hoodoo man, had let him come charging right through her ranks, and now he, as well as her father, was now safely behind them.

Her scouts had preformed their tasks perfectly, and now no barriers lay between the horde and the town. What was left of the police force was also behind her rear flank, though the sheriff was conspicuously absent. That fact did not worry her, however. She would find him in good time, and then he would pay for what he had done to her.

She had not wanted to see her father, so she had stayed back, away from the road. If she had glimpsed him, she might have experienced a feeling of longing, a moment of weakness which she could ill afford. Now she would be able to concentrate on the task at hand: exterminating the town of the petty fools who had allowed the suffering of her and many others.

The lights of the town were now within sight. The horde was growing anxious; she could feel their eager hunger flowing all around her. Soon, it would be all but impossible to hold their bloodlust in check. She would be forced to release them from the tentative leash upon which she now held them and free them to attack with abandon.

There was the sound of gunfire from behind her. She had left a small group to guard the rear as they advanced. Surely the Hoodoo man was not so foolish as to try and attack them. His group was vastly outnumbered, and his weapons could not kill her minions.

But what if he were that foolish? And, worse, what if he were still dragging her father along? Whatever else happened, no harm could come to her father. Cynthia would not permit it. The others could die—*would* die—but her father was to remain untouched.

She paused, unsure whether to double back or continue on. A voice, unnaturally loud in the cool stillness of the night, made the decision for her.

"Cynthia!" Dave Baracheck called from the darkness. "Cynthie!"

Chapter Thirteen

"Keep calling," McCoy said to Baracheck. "We have to get her attention. She must know you're here."

Baracheck raised the bullhorn and called to his daughter once more. In the road ahead, barely visible in the faint moonlight, the Sluagh horde came into view. As before, they made no move to attack, but their small bodies trembled with unbridled anticipation. McCoy supposed that Cynthia Baracheck must have a very strong will to keep the creatures in check.

"Call again," he whispered. "We need to bring her out where we can see her." *And where she can see us*, he thought.

"Cynthie! Please come out! It's your father! It's *Daddy*!"

The center of the horde suddenly parted and Cynthia stepped out of the darkness. Big John blushed at the sight of her nakedness and looked at his shoes. Unnoticed by everyone but McCoy, Kenner gave a lewd smile of approval.

Baracheck either didn't notice her lack of clothing or dismissed it. He saw only his daughter, his precious little girl, taken from him so long ago. Tears welled in his eyes. He tried to speak, but all that came out was a weak choking noise.

Cynthia stared at her father, her expression unreadable. McCoy was not close enough to look into her eyes, but he sensed a storm of conflicting emotions raging within her. The Sluagh, perhaps sensing this as well, shifted about nervously.

"Go," she said, breaking the tense silence. "Go home, Father. I go to avenge us, for what was done to us. Go home. You will not be harmed."

Slowly, carefully, McCoy edged between Baracheck and Kenner. He nudged John, and when the big man looked at him, McCoy gave a slight flick of his head. *Move out of the way*, the gesture said. John, thankfully understanding, shuffled slowly to the side.

"Talk to her," McCoy said to Baracheck. "Try to reason with her."

Baracheck struggled to find his voice. "Cynthia," he said. "Please don't do this. We've suffered, you and I, but we can put that behind us now."

"Can we?" Cynthia asked haughtily. "I was bartered into slavery so the sheriff could keep his job. But I am a slave no more. These people need to be punished for their complacency. I am here to serve justice."

McCoy slipped his hand into his knapsack and felt around until his fingers settled on the item he was seeking. He eased the item out of the bag, being careful not to let any of the others notice.

"But most of those people are innocent," Baracheck argued. "If Sheriff Lyle is guilty of what you say, then he should be punished. None of these other people knew what was happening."

"The greatest crime is to stand and do nothing while injustice is taking place," Cynthia said. She shook her head like a stubborn girl. "I don't have time to argue the point. Just go. Go home and forget you even saw me."

McCoy unscrewed the cap from the bottle he was holding.

"How could I do that, Cynthia?" Baracheck asked. "I've been looking for you for seventeen years. *Seventeen years*. Do you think I could just walk away now?"

For a moment, Cynthia's stern expression faltered. In that split second, she was a little girl again, lost and alone and longing for her father. "Go home!" she yelled, almost pleading. "I don't want to see you get hurt!"

Now.

McCoy turned and splashed the holy water in Kenner's face. The small man howled as the consecrated liquid burned into his flesh, and he dropped to his knees and clawed at the burning skin. Everyone had been focused on the exchange between Baracheck and Cynthia, but now they turned to regard Kenner with puzzled looks.

"Ostendo vestri!" McCoy whispered, loud enough for Kenner to hear but too faint for anyone else to make out.

The demon gave a wail of pain and fury and tore itself from Kenner's body. As it had before, it assumed the fearsome canine-like visage. Amanda and Deidre gave startled cries. Big John's eyes grew to the size of soup bowls.

"Subsisto!" McCoy hissed. *Remain.* The word effectively bound the entity, preventing it from escaping to another plane.

The demon rose to its towering full height and glared at McCoy. It threw back its head and uttered and unearthly howl.

"Enjoying your ringside seat to my demise?" McCoy whispered. Before the demon could respond, McCoy ducked behind Baracheck, to the coal mines. It wasn't that bad, really, and he knew that he was lucky to have a job at all.

When there was enough coffee in the carafe to fill his mug, he snatched the pot and quickly sloshed the joe into his cup. Some of the hot liquid poured onto the warmer before he could replace the carafe, but that was okay. He only had time for one cup, anyway. He wished he had more time to relish the stillness of the early morning, but he just couldn't bring himself to wake up any earlier. At least he didn't have to work the hoot owl shift anymore. That had gotten really old really quick.

From somewhere outside, his dog Rusty began to bark. That was just great. The dumb mutt would probably end up waling Carolyn, and Sam would just as soon not have that happen. Not that he wouldn't like to get a kiss goodbye before he left, but Carolyn tended to be grumpy as hell if something woke her before she was ready to get up.

Rusty was really tearing it up out there. Sam wondered what was causing the dog to cut such a shine. Maybe it was because he hadn't been awake for long, but he was starting to feel on edge. He considered the shotgun in the hall closet, and suddenly thought that he would like very much to have it in his hands. The feeling was totally ungrounded, but that didn't make it any less urgent. He trotted to the closet and retrieved the firearm.

"What's up with Rusty?" Carolyn called from the bedroom, her voice thick with sleep.

"Nothing," Sam answered. "I'm going out to check on him. Go back to sleep."

He waited a moment for a response, and when there was none he eased toward the kitchen door. He flipped the switch to the porch light, knowing as soon as he did it that it was a wasted effort. The bulb had blown weeks ago. He'd been meaning to replace it, but had never gotten around to it.

If he took the time to rummage around for a new bulb, replace the blown one, and go check on things outside, he would be late for work. He remembered that there was a flashlight in the kitchen junk drawer, the one beside the refrigerator, and he grabbed it. The batteries were weak, but it would shine enough light to let him see where he was going.

He was unlocking the door when he realized that Rusty had stopped barking. When had that happened? When he was getting the gun? The flashlight? He wasn't sure. Maybe it had just been a coyote passing close enough for Rusty to pick up its scent. Probably that was it, who was still holding the shotgun in one hand. "Holy God! Shoot that thing, Dave!"

Baracheck, as stunned as the others over the demon's sudden appearance, nonetheless raised the firearm and blasted a round at the evil entity. Since demons are not particularly susceptible to iron, this served only to piss the entity off. It swung a massive, clawed hand at Baracheck. McCoy, ready for the move, grabbed the back of Baracheck's shirt and pulled. The demon's swipe missed Baracheck by inches, and the startled man tumbled to the ground.

From her vantage point, Cynthia saw the demon materialize. She had never seen such a creature before, but she knew that it was not Fey. She watched as the cowardly Hoodoo man ducked behind her father, saw her father fire at the beast, and looked on in horror as the monster struck her father down.

"Daddy!" she screamed. She looked to her minions and pointed to the demon. "Attack! Kill!"

The Sluagh responded fiercely, partly because their Queen had ordered it, but also because they saw this newcomer as a threat to their newfound position in the Fey hierarchy. They swarmed the surprised demon, literally climbing over each other in an attempt to latch onto a body part and sink their sharp teeth into the fiend's flesh. The demon, trapped in a corporeal form, was vulnerable to their attacks.

Vulnerable or not, the entity was far from defenseless. While the Sluagh were technically Fey, their grotesque little bodies housed mortal souls, and this made them fair game for the flailing demon. With an otherworldly wail, the fiend released a circle of hellfire. All of the Sluagh within a five foot radius fell to the ground, their fragile souls shattered and their bodies, which had reverted back to their human forms, burnt beyond recognition. Unfortunately for the demon, three dozen more Sluagh surged forth to take the place of their fallen comrades.

As the battle raged, McCoy helped Baracheck to his feet and assayed the man for any damage.

"I'm okay," Baracheck assured him. He looked in awe at the demon. "What the hell is that thing?"

"Exactly," McCoy answered. "Hell being the operative word." He picked up the shotgun and tossed it to John, who barely tore his eyes away from the spectacle before him long enough to catch it.

"Get ready," McCoy said. "There are hundreds of Sluagh, and only one little demon. We're still gonna have a fight on our hands."

Amanda walked over and hit McCoy in the arm. It was not a love lick.

"The next time you come up with some half-baked plan," she said, "how about a little advance warning? I nearly peed my pants when that thing showed up."

"Be mad at me later. Right now, help me with those trash bags."

They each grabbed a bag. Amanda let out a surprised gasp and nearly dropped hers.

"Something's moving in there!" she hissed at McCoy.

He nodded. "We're close now. They can sense the Sluagh."

"What can sense the Sluagh?"

"The poppets. Hold on tight. Don't let any of them out. Not just yet."

"Let them out? They're little dolls made out of grass."

"Keep telling yourself that. Any minute now Cynthia is going to realize she's been tricked. When I tell you to, dump the poppets out. Not before. Once that's done, grab a gun and stay close to me."

"You're a hell of a date, Finn McCoy."

"I bet you tell all the handlers that."

Amanda looked genuinely surprised.

"There are others?" she asked.

***

With a greater relief than she would have expected, Cynthia saw that her father was unharmed. She almost ran to him, but then she remembered her place and stood her ground.

Returning her attention to the battle before her, she saw that her forces were gaining the upper hand. The monster's retaliatory strikes were becoming weaker and less frequent. Still, she had lost dozens, and would perhaps lose dozens more before victory was theirs. She felt no remorse for the fallen Sluagh; in truth, she loathed them nearly as much as the people of the town. But at least they had not rejected her, and had, in fact, made her their Queen. That gesture alone placed them a few rungs higher on the ladder than the cold, heartless townspeople.

She glanced at her father again. She could have sworn that he had been struck by the monster, the way he had fallen when it had swung at him. Perhaps he had taken a lucky fall at just the right moment.

Or perhaps the Hoodoo man had jerked her father out of the way. Why would he do that, when he had been cringing so cowardly behind her father only moments before?

Her eyes began to dart back and forth between her father, the Hoodoo man, and the monster.

It had been a trick. It had all been planned. She had fallen for it as blindly as the little girl she'd been when the Sluagh had taken her away. And now she was depleting her forces on a senseless attack while the Hoodoo man sat idly by and watched.

With a cry of fury, Cynthia began to sprint toward the Hoodoo man and his group, her plans for the town and even concern for her father's safety temporarily forgotten. The remaining Sluagh who were not actively involved in fighting the demon raced behind her, bloodlust tingeing their bulging black eyes.

***

"Now!" McCoy shouted, and he and Amanda dumped the poppets onto the dew-covered ground. As soon as they were free of the bags, the little dolls began to shake and squirm as if the earth beneath them were trembling violently.

"Time for some magic," McCoy said.

"I really can't take much more," Deidre said as she stared at the dolls. "I've seen more in the past few hours than I ever wanted to."

"Stay focused," John told her, but he was also watching the poppets with an uneasy eye.

As the Sluagh charged closer, the poppets' movements increased dramatically. They began to mutate, their brittle little bodies growing and elongating. Grass and straw was replaced with skin and fur. The heads, featureless except for two black stones which served as eyes, began to grow snouts and mouths with tiny, razor-sharp teeth. By the time the Sluagh had crossed half the distance to the group, the poppets had morphed into creatures which resembled small but extremely vicious and pissed-off baboons.

"I dreamt about this," Baracheck said. His voice sounded faraway, and his eyes had a vacant look as he gazed upon the things he had come to know as grass monkeys. "I saw them changing in my sleep."

"Earth to Dave," McCoy said urgently. "You need to get back here, right now. There's no guarantee that Cynthia will be able to protect you during this."

Baracheck shook his head as if coming out of a deep slumber. He looked at McCoy and nodded.

Almost as a single entity, the poppet/monkeys charged the oncoming Sluagh onslaught. The front of the Sluagh line slowed as the fairies recognized the fray's new combatants; they had not been prepared to face this ancient magic. Some of them actually stopped, but the majority of the horde kept coming, albeit with considerably less enthusiasm as before.

"How did you do that?" John asked McCoy. "How did you make them change?"

"I didn't. The magic was in the poppets themselves. Whoever made them put it there."

"Dalton said she was Native American," Baracheck said as he watched the spectacle with amazement. "Cherokee, I think."

"That would make sense," McCoy agreed. "Native American magic is based on elemental nature. They probably started making these things centuries ago."

Cynthia saw the monkeys coming, but it was too late to do anything about it. For a brief moment, she remembered playing with a similar doll as a child. But her mother had thrown it away, and the Sluagh had come for her soon after. When they had taken her from her room, her mother had been there, but she had done nothing to try to save Cynthia. She had just sat there on the bed, as still as a mannequin, and done nothing.

Her dear father had tried to save her, but he had been too late. He had never given up on her, though. He had scoured the woods and forests all these years, searching for her, never giving up hope.

Was this how she was going to repay him?

Cynthia faltered, then slowed, then came to a stop. She stood looking at her father, saw the age in his face, the way his posture stooped more than she remembered, and she wondered what she was doing. Throughout all she'd been through, there had been someone who had never stopped loving her and whose only wish was to have her back in his life. She could have gone to him many times, but she'd been so blinded by hatred that she had failed to see the only avenue that mattered, that made any sense at all.

Suddenly, with the force of an avalanche, Cynthia wanted her Daddy. She wanted the madness to be over, wanted nothing except to be held in his protective arms, to let him stroke her hair and tell her everything was going to be all right.

But now she had put him in danger. She needed to get to him, to stand beside him and protect him from any member of the horde which might try to attack him.

"Daddy!" she yelled, and took off at a sprint just as the Sluagh and the magical poppets collided in a frenzied mass of shrill cries and gnashing teeth.

***

Unnoticed by the humans, who were now watching the battle between the Sluagh and the poppets, the demon had silently gained the upper hand in its own battle. With the majority of the horde now engaged on the other front, the entity was able to slay enough of its foes to gain some breathing room. It was hurt, yes, but it was far from being vanquished. It also found renewed strength in the one task that it wanted to perform before McCoy banished it back to its own plane.

It wanted to kill the bitch that had sicced the bloody fairies on it.

The fiend knew that it had no hope of hurting McCoy, not in its present weakened state. The man had too much magical protection. If it had been stronger, perhaps, but even then the outcome would be questionable. The girl, however, possessed no special protection at all. Since escape was not an option thanks to McCoy's binding spell, the demon could at least relish in one final kill before it was banished.

It fried the last of its attackers with one final, powerful burst of hellfire. Its magic was nearly spent, but that would not matter now. It still owned a powerful body with sharp teeth and nasty claws, and it had just enough energy to close the distance on the girl and rip her to shreds.

The girl was presently running toward McCoy's group, a worried expression on her face. Apparently, she had undergone a change of heart and now wished to join the other humans. That was too bad.

She would never make it.

The demon smiled and launched itself at the unsuspecting girl.

***

McCoy watched the pitched battle between the Sluagh and the poppets with only slightly less awe than the others. He had seen a lot during his lifetime, but this was definitely a first. The monkeys were outnumbered about two to one, but their magical origins and aggressive fighting style made them more than a match for the evil fairies.

Still, the numbers were on the side of the Sluagh. They would probably overwhelm the poppets at some point, but McCoy was hoping that their ranks would be decimated enough to allow he and the others to finish the job with their iron-loaded firearms. Between the poppets and the demon, the ranks of the Sluagh had dwindled enough that McCoy was fairly certain they would have little trouble disposing of the remaining fairies.

As he thought of the demon, he glanced in the direction of the other battle to see how it was progressing. To his surprise, he saw that the demon had vanquished its Sluagh attackers and was now moving quickly across the field. His eyes followed the entity's projected path and he was even more surprised to see Cynthia running toward them. At first, he thought that she was on the attack, but then he saw that her attention was on her father, and he saw the fear and concern on her face.

Something had snapped within her, and now she was just a frightened young woman running to the aid of her father.

Unfortunately, she was also about to become breakfast for a maddened demon.

Uttering a silent curse, McCoy dropped his walking stick and raced to intercept the rapidly advancing fiend.

Chapter Fourteen

Amanda saw McCoy take off at a sprint out of the corner of her eye. She turned and saw him, Cynthia, and the demon. It took her only a second to realize what was happening.

"Finn!" she screamed. "No!"

McCoy paid her no heed. He raced toward the demon, which was only moments away from reaching the girl. Cynthia, her attention fixated on her father, had not even realized the danger she was in.

Baracheck, alerted by Amanda's scream, turned and saw what was happening.

"Cynthie!" he yelled. "Cynthie, look out!"

Cynthia heard her father shout and followed his gaze. At first, she saw the Hoodoo man racing toward her and thought that he meant to intercept her, but then she turned her head a little further and saw a massive shape closing in. Startled, she tripped and went sprawling to the ground just as the demon lunged at her.

The demon saw her go down, but it was already committed, in mid-flight. Trapped as it was in its corporeal form, it had no choice but to follow the laws of physics. It knew it was going to miss on the first pass, but that would be all right. It could turn as it landed and be upon her before she had a chance to get back to her feet.

Even as the demon thought this, something slammed into it, changing its trajectory and plowing it into the ground. The entity turned its head to see McCoy, winded but irate, scrambling to get on top of it.

"McCoy!" the demon growled, enraged to see that the bane of its earthly existence was trying to step between it and its prey. The demon had thought earlier that it had little chance of beating McCoy because it had assumed the man would never allow it to get close enough for a physical attack. Now that the two were grappling in close quarters, however, all bets were off.

The entity snapped its head forward in an attempt to bite McCoy, but the handler deftly dodged the attack and planted a punch of his own on the demon's snout. The fiend wailed in rage and pain. It struggled to get out from under the pesky human and mount its own attack.

Cynthia had been frozen by the spectacle taking place on the ground beside her. Shaking herself out of her daze, she jumped to her feet and ran to her father. She fell into his arms, sobbing with relief. Baracheck held her tightly and stroked her hair.

"It'll be okay," he told her. "I promise you, it'll be okay."

Amanda turned to John. ""I'm going to help Finn. You and Deidre watch those two."

John nodded. He turned and surveyed the battlefield. The fighting was intense and the combatants were dropping fast. It would soon be over, and from the looks of things there would still be some Sluagh to deal with. He motioned Deidre closer and they positioned themselves between the fray and the newly reunited father and daughter.

Amanda stopped long enough to grab McCoy's knapsack. She quickly rifled through it, but doing so did her little good. She didn't know what most of the items were, and had no idea which, if any, might be effective against a demon. She cursed herself for not having learned more in the previous six months. With a squeal of frustration, she closed the knapsack and ran toward McCoy.

***

McCoy realized he was in a tight spot. If he could put some distance between him and the demon and get a little breathing room, he would be able to banish the fiend with little trouble. As it was, locked in hand-to-hand combat with the entity, it would be nearly impossible to do. He was constantly having to dodge the demon's teeth and claws, and more than once he had narrowly escaped being disemboweled by the thinnest of margins.

Physically, they were pretty evenly matched. The demon was drastically weakened from its fight with the Sluagh, while McCoy was fairly fresh and rested. Had the entity's strength not been drained, it would have been able to easily overpower McCoy. The outcome of this battle hinged on which one would tire first. McCoy knew that his age and lack of exercise put him at a disadvantage, but he fought on determinedly, hoping for an opening that would allow him to escape the demon's clutches and escape.

Something came swishing through the air and caught the demon squarely in the face. It howled, spun around to see what had attacked it, and caught another blow to the head for its trouble. There stood Amanda, her feet set wide apart, swinging McCoy's walking stick like the Queen of the Home Run Derby. Her blue eyes were wild, and the look of manic ferocity on her face struck fear into both the demon and McCoy.

Rolling away from the demon's clutches, McCoy sprang to his feet, ready to work the banishing spell and put an end to this nonsense. The entity, however, had refocused its attention on Amanda. She was still swinging wildly with the cane, but her blows were bouncing harmlessly off the demon's muscled shoulders and torso.

"Amanda!" McCoy shouted. "Get back! Get out of there!"

Whether she didn't hear or chose to ignore him, Amanda wound up for another mighty swing.

The demon, however, had recovered for its initial surprise. It easily dodged Amanda's strike and backhanded her with enough force to send her flying. She crumpled to the ground and lay unmoving.

"No!" screamed McCoy. The banishing spell forgotten, he rushed in, meaning to put himself between the fiend and the fallen Amanda. But the demon was ready for him. It spun and launched itself at McCoy, hitting him low and buckling his legs. He felt the left one break with a sickening snap.

McCoy hit the ground in a blinding flash of pain. Large, black orbs danced before his eyes and obstructed his field of vision. He tried to rise to one elbow but the demon pushed him back, its wicked claws piercing his skin and drawing blood.

"It seems the day is mine, after all," the entity cackled. "I told you your time was done!"

With a shrill laugh, the demon reared back and prepared to deliver the death blow.

***

"They're coming!" Deidre cried. She squeezed off a round from McCoy's 9mm and a Sluagh hit the ground dead, its body reverting to its former human form.

The Sluagh had finally destroyed all of the poppets, but at a great cost to their numbers. Between the poppets and the battle with the demon, perhaps twenty to thirty of the evil fairies remained. With McCoy and Amanda gone, it was left up to John and Deidre to protect the Barachecks and destroy what remained of the horde. With the ammo that they had, it was going to be a tall order.

"Keep behind us," John told the father and daughter. He looked toward the spot where McCoy and Amanda had gone, but he couldn't really see anything in the gloom. Shapes, maybe, but it was difficult to tell what was happening.

"Can you make them go away?" Deidre asked Cynthia.

The young woman shook her head. "They won't listen to me now. I've betrayed them. They'll kill me just as quickly as the rest of you."

"No one's going to die," Baracheck assured his daughter.

"I hope you're right," John said. He fired a round from his shotgun and managed to take down two of the Sluagh.

"How's your ammo holding out?" Deidre asked.

"I'm down to six shots, I think. Maybe five. You?"

"One clip after this one."

"Make them count, then."

They eased backwards, across the field and toward the road. The Sluagh followed at a respectful distance, since they had seen that the humans' weapons could actually kill them. John had hoped that since there were so few of them left they might flee back into the woods, but the little fairies seemed to be more determined than ever.

"Which way?" Baracheck asked when they reached the road. "Back to the truck or back toward town?"

"Neither," John replied. "We don't know if we could get the truck started. And McCoy and Amanda are out there somewhere. We're not leaving without them."

"So we just stand here and wait for them to attack us?"

John looked at the sky, which was beginning to brighten along the eastern horizon.

"What will they do when the sun rises?" he asked Cynthia.

She shrugged. "They want blood. I don't think the light will stop them."

"I wish we had that other shotgun," Deidre said.

"So do I," John agreed. "I lost it in the excitement. Maybe McCoy or Amanda has it, I don't know."

"There's a fog rising," Baracheck said, indicating the field. "I don't like it."

John looked out over the field. Sure enough, a white mist was blowing in rapidly from the direction of the woods. It was covering the field too quickly to be a natural occurrence.

"Something's happening," he whispered.

The Sluagh seemed to sense it too. They repeatedly glanced behind them, and they began to chatter amongst themselves in hushed but urgent tones.

"We should go," Baracheck said.

John shook his head stubbornly. "I told you, we're not leaving without the others. McCoy's the only reason we've made it this far. I'm not going to leave him behind."

Suddenly the argument became moot. The Sluagh, having come to some mutual agreement between themselves, charged the group. The deputies, caught off guard, were slow to raise and fire their weapons. Nonetheless, between the two of them they were able to drop nearly a dozen more of the creatures before they reached the group.

They went for Deidre first, avoiding John because of his size. Several of them managed to get under her feet and trip her up, sending her tumbling to the pavement. She struck her head on the hard surface and went limp.

One of then climbed on her chest and went for her exposed throat, but in a single stride John was there. He grabbed the creature by the scruff of its neck and pulled it off the fallen woman. It turned on him, clawing and biting, but then it seemed to get a whiff of something. Its expression went from rage to bewilderment and then, finally, to terror. Instead of trying to attack John, it began to struggle to get away from him.

John gripped the Sluagh tightly as it tried desperately to escape. Suddenly, a purplish fire sprang from his hands and engulfed the terrified creature. It gave a final wail as the flames consumed it, then it fell from John's grasp. It hit the ground, little more than charred flesh and bones.

John stared dumbly at his hands. The fire was gone. The remaining Sluagh regarded him with awe and horror. Almost as one, they turned tail and scurried back up the road, away from town.

"Fairy fire!" Cynthia gasped, her expression unbelieving. She looked at John. "You're Fey!"

John shook his head violently. "No!" he said. "I don't know what that was, but I'm not *anything*! I'm just me!"

"You wield the fire!" Cynthia insisted. She shrank back against her father, who was eying John with suspicion.

John took a step toward them, palms out, and they both retreated. Baracheck defensively pulled his daughter closer.

"You've got to believe me," John pleaded. "I don't know what that was, but it's never happened before. I'm as human as you. I grew up here, went to school. I'm not a monster!"

Cynthia looked into his eyes and seemed to relax a little. "Maybe not a monster," she said. "But not human, either. Not fully."

"It's not possible," John said, still looking down at his hands.

"Did you know your parents?" Baracheck asked. "You weren't adopted, were you?"

"Adopted? No. My mother passed away several years ago, but my Dad still lives in town. Over on Greene Street. He's as normal as anyone, and so was my Mom."

"Still," Cynthia said, "you have the fire. Humans don't."

John shook his head again. He didn't have any answers. He didn't feel any different than he had five minutes ago, other than being scared to death.

Deidre let out a low moan. John turned to her, cursing himself for having forgotten about his fallen comrade. He rushed to her side just as her eyes flitted open.

"Ow, my head," she mumbled. She looked up at John. "What did I miss?"

John turned and looked at Baracheck and Cynthia, his eyes pleading.

"Nothing, really," Baracheck said. "They were attacking, then something scared them off. Don't know what."

John shot the man a look of gratitude. He didn't want anyone to know about this, least of all the people he worked with.

"Think you can walk?" he asked Deidre. "We need to find the others."

"I think so. Anyone know where they are?"

As if in answer, an unearthly scream split the early morning silence.

It had come from the mist-shrouded field.

***

McCoy blinked furiously as he tried to clear his vision. If this was the end, he at least wanted to see it coming.

At first, he thought that maybe he'd gone blind. That wasn't right, though. Everything was white, not black. If he'd gone blind, everything should be black. Then he realized he was looking into a dense fog. That was strange. He didn't recall the fog being there only moments ago, but then most of his attention had been focused on his broken leg and pierced chest, so it was entirely possible that he could have missed something.

He realized that he actually should be dead by now and wondered what the demon was waiting for. Was it simply toying with him? Probably. Demons were like that, after all. Damn, his leg hurt.

There was a sudden scream from somewhere very close by. McCoy's first thought was of Amanda. Could that be the reason that the demon hadn't finished him off yet? Was it torturing Amanda, intent on forcing McCoy to witness her demise before receiving his own?

With a grunt of agony, he rolled over and forced himself up on his elbows. Between the pain and the fog, he was unable to get his bearings. Still, he couldn't just lay there and do nothing. He began to crawl awkwardly into the mist, eyes searching and ears straining to hear the slightest sound.

From his left came another howl, followed by the sound of someone or something thrashing about. McCoy veered in that direction, going as fast as he could but still moving at an agonizingly slow pace. If the demon had hurt Amanda, he was going to kill it. He wasn't sure how, given his present condition, but with God as his witness he would find a way.

He was close now. He could hear movement just ahead of him, the sounds of struggle. At least Amanda was fighting back. McCoy redoubled his efforts. He could not bear to lose her, though he had no idea how he might be able to save her.

The fog suddenly thinned, and McCoy beheld a sight which he had never dreamed of witnessing, not if he lived a thousand years. There before him was the demon, its limbs and head entangled in a swarming mass of roots and branches, which were slowly but surely pulling the fiend into the soft earth. The entity shook as it tried in vain to free itself and gave off weak bursts of hellfire, which were ineffective since there was no human soul to consume.

McCoy's head was spinning, both from the pain of his injuries and the spectacle before him. On a small stump beside him, a face appeared briefly. It gave him a wry smile, then vanished.

The dryad gave a sudden, violent jerk, and the demon disappeared into the earth. Nothing remained to suggest it had ever been there.

McCoy rolled onto his back and chuckled softly. The whole thing was ridiculous. He had just been saved from a demon—by the Fey. If he had looked up and seen a herd of pigs flying overhead, he would not have been surprised.

Something moved beside him, but he didn't have the energy to turn and see what it was. There was a gasp, and then Amanda's face loomed over him. Her cheek was red and already beginning to bruise, and her expression was one of shock and concern.

"Finn? Oh my God! Finn, can you hear me?"

"See them pigs flyin'?" he asked. His leg had gone numb, but he was having trouble breathing. He thought that a lung might be punctured.

There was the sound of hurried footsteps approaching, but he couldn't see who it was. There was some loud discussion that he couldn't seem to make out. Something about a hospital, maybe. His vision was fading, but suddenly Amanda's face came into view again. She was leaning close, and she had tears in her eyes.

"Don't you die, you big galoot," she said. "Hang on. Hang on for me. I love you."

He guessed he had known it, but it felt good to hear it, just the same.

"I love you, too," he whispered, and then the world faded away to black.

Chapter Fifteen

McCoy woke to a very bright light, but the strong smell of ammonia and other disinfectants assured him that he was in a hospital, not the hereafter. It took a few moments for his eyes to adjust and focus. When they did, he saw Big John Talbot grinning at him.

"Well, look who's awake," the big man said. He moved closer to McCoy's bed, trying to hide his concern under an outwardly jovial manner. "I was starting to think you were going to sleep for a week."

"How long was I out?" McCoy asked, or tried to. His voice was raspy and his throat was raw. Evidently, something had recently been stuffed down his gullet.

"Two days," John replied. "Doc says the chest wounds are nothing to worry about. Superficial scratches, mainly. The leg's a mess, though."

"You're putting me on."

"Amanda's been here since we brought you in. I finally convinced her to go get something to eat."

McCoy nodded. "Good. We need to talk, anyway. I didn't really get a chance to go over the cover story with you."

John held up his hand and shook his head. "Already taken care of. We were lucky. A few of the bodies we recovered of the...Sluagh, I think Amanda called them...were of folks who had disappeared recently, within the past several months. We placed those in a few strategic spots and blamed the whole mess on them." The happy look he'd been forcing for McCoy's benefit vanished, replaced by a frown. "It worked, the state boys bought it. But I've got to tell you, I'm not thrilled about placing the blame on innocent people. I mean, it's got to be hard on their families."

"I understand," McCoy said. "When I get up and about, we'll pay a visit to those families, talk about the influence of cults, and tell them their loved ones were most likely drugged and not acting on their own violation. I know it's not much, but it's about all we can do." He gave the big man a long look. "To tell the truth, I'm kind of surprised you went along with the whole cover-up thing."

John looked away. Under normal circumstances, he would have balked at lying to the state police, much less being actively involved in a cover-up. But the event with the fairy fire a few days ago had changed things. He could not afford to go blabbering about evil fairies and other supernatural stuff when there was a real chance that he harbored a dark secret of his own. He didn't want anyone to find out, and the way things stood presently, he didn't think they would.

"Amanda talked me into it," he said. "She told me about the truce you made with the Fey. I'm just acting in the best interests of the people I'm sworn to protect."

"Any sign of Lyle?" McCoy asked.

John shook his head. "Not a word. He's dead, I know. I should feel bad, but I don't. Not really. Not if he was in league with those monsters."

"Do you think he was?"

"I'm pretty sure he was. It all adds up. The council will appoint an interim sheriff soon. Some folks think it will be me."

"I'm sure it will," McCoy said. "I'll vouch for you."

John smiled. "Thanks. It will mean a lot, coming from you."

"I don't know about that," McCoy said.

"Oh. I forgot. You don't know how big of a hero you are. Pretty much saved the day single-handedly."

McCoy groaned. "What have you done, John?"

"Just told the truth," the big man grinned. "Omitting, of course, any mention of fairies and magical dolls and demons." His eyes went wide as he remembered something. "That reminds me. How did you know the demon was in Kenner?"

"I didn't, not until we were riding out to meet the Sluagh, when he was sitting beside me in the truck. I'd been too distracted to notice. But when he started grilling me on how I could sense things, I began to put two and two together. The way he was still walking around with an obviously mortal wound, for instance. I'd had a run-in with the same demon a day or so before, and it had promised me it would be there when I met my end." He looked down at the bandages covering his chest and his battered leg, which was in a cast and raised on a pulley. "It almost fulfilled that promise."

"What happened to the demon?" John asked. "It was gone when we got there."

"I managed to banish it," McCoy lied. Big John would be learning a lot in the weeks to come, and the last thing he wanted was for the big man to think that the Fey had any capacity for kindness. The dryad had saved McCoy because it needed him for something else, nothing more. It had not been an altruistic act on the fairy's part.

"What happened to Dave and Cynthia?" McCoy asked.

"Gone. They lit out yesterday. I think they were planning on going back to Knoxville, maybe. Try to start again where no one really knows them."

"I hope it works out for them."

"Me too."

The door opened and Amanda walked in looking weary and haggard. When she saw that McCoy was awake, she dropped her purse and ran to his side. She grabbed his neck and hugged him tightly. It hurt like hell, but McCoy stifled a yell and managed to escape with a soft grunt.

"Sorry!" she said as she let go of him. "Did I hurt you?"

"No. I'm good," he lied again.

"Oh, Finn!" Tears welled in her eyes. "You don't know how worried I was. I thought I was going to lose you. What were you thinking, tackling that demon the way you did?"

"What was *I* thinking?" McCoy asked incredulously. "Who was the one swinging my walking stick like Babe Ruth?" He looked at her face. She'd covered it with makeup, but he could still see the bruising underneath. His tone softened. "You can't be doing that, Amanda. If that thing had used its claws instead of the back of its hand...I don't even want to think about it. I couldn't lose you, either. It would be the end of me."

Her lower lip started trembling, and he braced himself for another hug attack. Sure enough, it came, knocking the wind out of him. He hugged her back though, as best he could, and it felt wonderful.

"I'd better be going," John said, looking a trifle embarrassed.

"Hold on," McCoy said as Amanda once again released him from the death grip. "One more thing I need to tell you. Come close."

John walked over and lowered his ear toward McCoy's mouth. McCoy whispered six words. John raised his head and looked questioningly at him, but McCoy just smiled and turned his attention back to Amanda. John left the room puzzled, but he was sure his new friend wouldn't leave him in the dark for long.

"The doctor says it may be a while before you run your next marathon," Amanda said.

"That's okay. I was thinking of taking a break from them, anyway. I hope you didn't break my walking stick."

Amanda nodded across the room. McCoy followed her gaze and saw the stick leaning against the wall.

"And my knapsack?" he asked.

"In the closet with your clothes. What's left of them."

"Oh God. Tell me my hat's okay."

"Don't worry. It doesn't look any worse than it already did."

"I'll ignore that. What about Boo?"

"Unfortunately, John had it towed into town. They're working on it, at the town's expense."

"Well, I hope they're gentle with him."

"Finn?"

"Yes?"

"Will you promise me something?"

"If I can."

"When you're up and able, can we go somewhere, just the two of us?"

"Sure. Where would you like to go?"

"Somewhere where there aren't any mountains or forests. Definitely somewhere where there are no Fey. The beach, maybe. How about that?"

He scrunched his nose. "I dunno. I burn easily."

"Finn!"

"Okay, okay. I guess I could use a break. The beach it is."

"Thank you," she said, not knowing how much she would later rue making the request. She gave him a big, sloppy kiss which ended only when the doctor entered the room, and even then only after he'd stood there several minutes, coughing loudly with embarrassment.

Epilogue

John Talbot took a pitcher from the refrigerator and poured himself a glass of iced tea. It was the same refrigerator he had raided as a ravenous teenager, possibly the same one he'd struggled mightily to open as a youngster. He couldn't be sure about that, but he knew this particular model had been serving the Talbot household for the last twenty years, at least.

"You want some tea, Dad?" he asked his father.

Guy Talbot shook his head. "I drink more than two glasses a day, I'm up pissing all night." He looked with pride upon his only son. John had always said he was going to be a cop, and he had made good on that promise. Now, he was also a hero, and to top that off, probably the next sheriff.

"I didn't catch you at a bad time, did I?" John asked.

"No, of course not. I'm glad you stopped by. Have you heard anything from the town council yet?"

John took a seat at the round kitchen table. "It'll probably be tomorrow."

"Well, it's a foregone conclusion, the way I see it."

"I guess so. Dad, I know this is going to sound funny, but did anything strange ever happen to you and Mom? I mean, like, before I was born?"

"Strange? What are you talking about?"

John tossed up his hands. "I don't know. Anything out of the ordinary, I guess. Did you see anything odd? Hear strange noises? See a flying saucer?"

Guy laughed. "Son, I don't know what you're looking for, but me and your Momma were about the two most normal, boring folks around. Ask anybody. Flying saucers, geesh."

"Yeah," John said, more than a little embarrassed. "I guess it was a stupid question."

"The only excitement we ever had was that time your mother got lost in the woods. Now, that wasn't strange, but it sure the hell was scary. For me, at least."

John perked up. "Mom got lost in the woods? When?"

"I don't know. A year or so before you were born, I think. Yeah, it must have been, because we were living on Miller's Ridge then. We moved to town right before she had you, so we would be closer to the hospital."

John's heart sank. He really didn't want to hear anymore, but he knew that he had to listen.

"I was working out at the Cold Ridge mines," his father continued. "I was on the hoot owl shift, and when I got home that morning, Tessa was nowhere to be found. I'd left her in the house the night before, and I always locked the doors before I left, but when I got there the front door was standing wide open."

"I'll bet you were freaking out," John said. He felt like he'd just swallowed a sizeable rock.

"Son, you don't know the half of it. I went through the house and checked all the rooms, but there was no sign of her. We had a little dog at the time, a Jack Russell named Puddles, and she was missing, too."

"I don't remember that dog," John said.

"No, you wouldn't. We never saw her again. Tessa turned back up, though, about three that afternoon. She'd heard Puddles barking the night before and had gone out to check on her. She'd gone out on the porch just in time to see the dog take off lickety-split into the woods. Of course, Tess being Tess, she followed the mutt. Got lost and spent all night and half the next day wandering around in those woods, trying to find her way back."

"And she just came walking back in the next day?"

"Yep," Guy gave a sad little laugh, the one he always gave when talking about his wife. "Of course, this was after I had the sheriff and half the town out looking for her. Embarrassed the hell out of her."

"Do you remember what time of the year it was?" John asked.

"Well, it was warm, thank God. If it had been during the winter, she likely would have frozen to death. But it was late summer. August, I think."

John had been born in May. He did the math in his head. It added up.

"That's some story," he said. "I don't think either of you ever mentioned it."

"I'd just about forgotten about it until you asked. That was a long time ago. Now, why don't you stay for supper? I'm no cook, but I'm sure I could round up something."

"I'll have to take a rain check," John said, rising. "Two of us are trying to cover the county right now. As soon as the council appoints me, *if* they do, I'll get some new deputies sworn in."

"You call me as soon as you find out," Guy said. He gave his son a big bear hug. "I'm awfully proud of you, John. I love you. You know that, right?"

"I know it, Dad. And I love you, too. We'll talk tomorrow."

John left the house and walked out to his cruiser. The day was as bright and beautiful as a mid-October day could be. On a day like this, it didn't seem possible that evil could exist in the world.

John had always wanted to be a cop, and nothing more than a cop. But he now knew that he was likely something more, and the thought unsettled him more than any other thought he'd ever had. He thought about the words McCoy had whispered in his ear. He wanted to take comfort in them, but he didn't know if he could.

You have a destiny to fulfill.

Big John Talbot climbed behind the wheel of his cruiser and drove off to be a cop, the only thing he'd ever wanted to be.

The End

Preview of Shadows in the Sand: A Finn McCoy Paranormal Thriller

Prologue

The moon was just rising above the outer rim of the sea when Stef Albright started her walk. The wind coming off the ocean was cool, and she shivered in spite of the fact she'd worn her sweater. Gulls and terns competed with pigeons for scraps of food left by beachgoers earlier in the day. The tourist season wouldn't start for another month or so, but there was a good share of locals who visited the beach on a daily basis, not to mention the odd vacationer who'd gotten a good deal on a beach house during the off season.

It wasn't like White Pine Island was a hub for the tourist crowd even during the peak of summer. It was more of a retirement community; the houses were older, the residents were older, and there were none of the gift shops and restaurants which littered every square inch of real estate up in Myrtle Beach. White Pine Island sat further off the beaten path, and the full-time residents liked it that way. A few of the houses were rental properties, but not many. Stef could remember a time when none of the houses were rentals, but times changed, and seldom for the better.

A gull circled her briefly as she walked, casing her for food, then went off in search of better prospects. In the distance, the fading light gleamed off a jet which was making its way to the airport in Myrtle. Stef's sandals splatted on the damp sand as she walked. Bob called them Jerusalem cruisers, and it never failed to make her laugh when he did so. This particular pair was looking kind of ragged. She made a mental note to pick up another pair the next time she went shopping.

She often wished that Bob would come with her on her evening walks, but her husband would rather sit on the balcony and watch the sun set with a glass of wine in his hand. True, it was sometimes nice to be alone with her thoughts, but Bob had been putting on weight in the past year or so, and a little bit of exercise wouldn't hurt him a single bit. Still, trying to get him to tag along was like trying to pull a sore tooth, and she had pretty much given up for the time being.

Steph's walk usually took her down to the pier and back unless she was really tired, in which case she only walked about half that distance before turning back. The total distance for a full trip was slightly less than two miles, and she never walked at a brisk pace, preferring instead to take her time and enjoy the sights and sounds of the ocean at sunset. This evening, she intended to go all the way to the pier before turning back toward home, unless the evening wind chilled her too much.

Her presence startled a group of terns, and they cajoled her for the intrusion. The sun was almost gone, a mere cuticle peeking above the dark waters of the ocean. The sound of the waves breaking against the beach was hypnotizing. Other than the ocean and the occasional cackling of the birds, the world was silent. The salty, sweet smell of the ocean filled her lungs as she walked. The wind began to pick up slightly, and it stung her bare legs with grains of sand and other debris.

She stopped as the sound of a radio drifted across the ocean breeze. She looked around for the source of the music but could not pinpoint it. As far as she could tell, she was alone on the beach. There were no houses nearby, and the pier was still half a mile in the distance. She listened more closely and decided that it wasn't a radio, after all. It sounded like someone singing. The voice was high, like a woman's voice, and the tune reminded her of a lullaby, or maybe an old blues tune by Billie Holiday. Stef couldn't make out the words, but they definitely had a sultry feel to them.

Puzzled, but not overly concerned, she continued her walk. Sounds had a way of behaving strangely on the beach. Likely, she was simply hearing the sound of someone singing from a distance.

She began to hum as she walked.

Near the water's edge, she could see several large shells glistening in the light of the rising moon. Slipping off her sandals, she walked across the wet sand and bent to examine them. One of them was broken and useless, but the other two appeared to be intact. She picked them up and slipped them into the pocket of her sweater.

She could still hear the singing, and she noticed that she was humming the exact same tune.

That was strange. The tune wasn't familiar to her; she was positive she hadn't heard it before. But here she was, humming along in perfect time and pitch. The singing seemed to be growing louder, as well. Or was that only a trick of the wind?

She gazed out over the dark ocean and saw someone in the water.

That was ridiculous. The water temperature was too cold this time of year for all but the most hardy of swimmers, and even then only in the daylight hours. Her eyes had to be deceiving her. She strained harder to make out the object. Surely it was nothing but a buoy or a large piece of debris. Whatever it was, it wasn't splashing around or making any motions that would indicate swimming. It looked, for all in the world, like someone treading water, their head and shoulders visible as they bobbed along with the ocean's current.

Though Steph could not make out any features, she could feel eyes upon her. Suddenly spooked, she stood and began retracing her steps back to her house. She was not in the mood to walk anymore. She simply wanted to return home and join Bob on the balcony, maybe even have a glass of wine herself. The night was getting too chilly, anyway.

She expected he singing to recede as she walked away, but if anything, it was getting louder. Slowing, she turned and looked back at the sea. The object she had seen was gone. Perhaps the tide had carried it further out. Or perhaps she hadn't really seen anything at all. The caps of the incoming waves could play tricks on the eyes.

She caught herself humming again and forced herself to stop. She didn't want to go back home with a case of the heebie-jeebies; Bob would never let her live it down. The moon was on the rise and it cast a soft illumination upon the beach. The waves danced and twinkled in its light.

Stef began to feel foolish. At fifty, she should have been well past the age of jumping at shadows. Here she was, in one of the most relaxing places in the world, and her nerves were wound up tighter than Dick's hatband.

The wine was sounding like a better idea all the time.

She was nearly home. The lights from the nearest houses were maybe a hundred yards away. The singing was growing louder, and she supposed it could be coming from this direction. Either someone in one of the houses was singing or they were listening to a radio or CD player. She could make out some of the words, but the song was being sung in a foreign language. It sounded like German, but since Steph didn't speak German, she couldn't be completely sure.

She looked back out at the ocean, saw nothing, and continued walking. There were more shells scattered along the beach here, and she scanned the sand under her feet for some more take-home treasures. Bob would fuss—there were shells piled up everywhere already—but he would get over it. She glanced at her shadow, looked back at her feet, and then froze in her tacks. She looked at her shadow again, and her breath caught in her throat.

Directly behind her shadow was another shadow. It was longer than her own, indicating a much taller person. When she had stopped, the other shadow had stopped as well.

Stef turned slowly and deliberately. She was not a large woman, but she had taken a few self-defense classes, and she had always thought that she could handle herself in a situation such as this. *The eyes and the groin*, she thought. *Always go for the eyes and the groin*. She remembered one of her instructors drilling that into her. *If they can't see and they can't walk, they can't chase you*.

There was a man standing behind her. He was smiling, he was naked, and he looked like the image of a Greek god carved into flesh-colored stone. His beauty was so stunning that Stef was taken aback. All vestiges of fear left her and she stood frozen, entranced by the man's mere presence. She felt as if she were suffocating, and she suddenly realized she was still holding her breath. She exhaled the stale air and took in a deep lungful of brine-tinged night.

The man said nothing, but the smile remained. He was tall, maybe six-two or six-three. His hair was dark and tousled, and his skin was a golden bronze. Stef had never before gazed upon anyone so perfect, male or female. She began to feel aroused, and was instantly ashamed. She tried to picture Bob, her husband of thirty years, and was inwardly horrified to find that she couldn't.

The man held out his hand as if inviting her to dance. She had no intention of taking this stranger's hand, and was amazed as she saw her own hand raise and slip delicately into his. The strange singing grew even louder, and her head started to spin. She felt drunk, euphoric. She hadn't felt this way since she'd tried marijuana back in college, and that had been many moons ago.

The man began to walk toward the ocean. He kept his head turned toward her, his eyes locked on hers, his smile hinting of things she had only dreamed about in her wildest schoolgirl fantasies. A part of her struggled to resist, but her mutinous body followed him anyway.

Hand in hand they walked into the ocean. She was vaguely aware of the chill of the water as the waves rushed against her bare feet and legs. Where were her sandals? She must have dropped them; she wasn't carrying them anymore. His hand felt much too cold, but whenever she tried to think about what that might imply, the singing grew louder still and her head swam even more.

They waded in up to their knees, then their waists. Stef was shivering so badly her teeth were chattering, but she could not take her eyes off his, and she could not stop walking. Soon the incoming waves were washing over her head, and still she walked, until her feet could no longer touch the sandy bottom. She swallowed a mouthful of saltwater and gagged violently. Their eyes never left each other's.

They began to move swiftly away from the beach. A small part of her, a part that was aware and screaming for the rest of her to wake up, realized that they were caught in a rip current. Her sweater and denim shorts were soaked, and she was having a hard time keeping hear head above water. He was still grasping her hand, but he made no attempt to aid her. He simply stared into her eyes and smiled.

She swallowed more brine. She could no longer keep her head above the water. They were both under now, and as she stared at him through the dark and churning water, she couldn't decide if his eyes were blue or green.

Green, she thought. *I do believe they're green.*

And then the darkness came and carried her away.

***

Available soon for purchase at the Amazon Kindle Store!

Made in the USA
Columbia, SC
12 February 2025